THE END OF ALL THINGS

THE END OF ALL THINGS

A LABYRINTH OF SOULS NOVEL

BY

MATTHEW LOWES

ShadowSpinners Press

This book is dedicated to everyone who has worked on and supported the *Labyrinth of Souls*, with special thanks to Josephe Vandel, Elizabeth Engstrom, Christina Lay, and all the LoST participants and authors. Thank you for making this all possible.

TABLE OF CONTENTS

Editor's Preface

Dungeon Solitaire: Labyrinth of Souls is a fantasy game for tarot cards, written by Matthew Lowes and Illustrated by Josephe Vandel. In the game you defeat monsters, disarm traps, open doors, and explore mazes as you delve the depths of a dangerous dungeon. Along the way you collect treasure and magic items, gain skills, and gather companions.

Now ShadowSpinners Press is publishing this and other stand-alone novels inspired by the game. Each *Labyrinth of Souls* novel features a journey into a unique vision of the underworld.

The Labyrinth of Souls is more than an ancient ruin filled with monsters, trapped treasure, and the lost tombs of bygone kings. It is a manifestation of a mythic underworld, existing at a crossroads between people and cultures, between time and space, between the physical world and the deepest reaches of the psyche. It is a dark mirror held up to human experience, in which you may find your dreams … or your doom. Entrances to this realm can appear in any time period, in any location. There are innumerable reasons why a person may enter, but it is a place antagonistic to those who do, a place where monsters dwell, with obstacles and illusions to waylay adventurers, and whose very walls can be a force of corruption. It is a haunted place, ever at the edge of sanity.

THE END OF ALL THINGS

1

GHOST CHATTER

Rithik crouched in the barren soil and shuffled toward the edge of the high escarpment. Below, across a flat plain crisscrossed with the faint traces of long buried roads, lay the city of dust. Since the end of the last age of the ancients, its high ceramite towers had slowly deteriorated into ruins, yet they still stood tall, silhouetted against the red glow of the setting sun.

He flicked a switch on the chatter box strapped to his wrist and held it close to the earth. It crackled to life as he waved the box across the rocky ground. Ghost chatter. There was a lot of it here, and there would be more in the desert beyond the city where he was headed. But that was the least of his worries. He was already doomed. The ghost flesh was in him. On his left forearm was a growing patch of purple skin. Thin tendrils of spreading infection reached as far as his shoulder, and when the ghost flesh consumed his heart or his head, he would cease to be.

There was no known treatment or cure, so death was his constant companion now. It was a cruel and terrible spirit, wiping out everything in its path, like the apocalypse of the world that was. His body would be eaten by animals, lions probably, but he would be gone. Sharo, the dream dweller, said his spirit would be carried westward by the great eagle Samsa, to the cave of the goddess Yananna. There he would be cleansed of world corruption and reborn into the next life.

That was all well and good as far as a dream dweller was concerned. They had karo tea to quell their fears. But Rithik couldn't escape death, and he couldn't accept it either. He was a hunter of Tavala, like his father. He would not go quietly into oblivion. That is not how the people of Tavala had survived for so long. He would struggle on until the bitter end, no matter how bitter.

He might have climbed a mountain or taken refuge in the forest and simply waited for death. But something in him wouldn't allow it. He had to have something to keep him going. So if Yananna held the secret to life and death, Rithik would not wait for Samsa to carry his spirit to her. He would go west now to seek her out. He would find her cave, plumb its depths, seek out the goddess, and know this secret for himself. That is what he would do.

He switched off the chatter box. Its power was running low and it didn't take a standard power cell. More importantly, he didn't have a standard power cell, and after years of use hunting for relics in the ruins of the river city, the power in his torch was gone. He would need the torch on his journey, and the city of dust was one of the few remaining places you might find the kind of standard cell it used. Unfortunately, the ruins were said to be crawling with tokmen.

He took a compact spyglass from the left chest pocket on his vest. He held it up to his eye and peered through it. A magnified view of the distance appeared in the circle of the spyglass. He scanned across the plain. In that otherwise barren expanse, a small ground hare caught his eye. He watched it for a moment, until it darted into its burrow by a tuft of scrub grass. Then he looked on toward the city.

The hollow shells of the ancient buildings were shrouded in darkness. He saw no movement, but the tokmen were there, somewhere. Maybe they were watching, even now. From ancient times the tokmen had fallen back into savagery. The evil that had laid waste to the world lived on in them. They could not be reasoned with. They could not be traded with. And they would not hesitate to kill and eat Rithik if they caught him in the city.

Rithik's left hand instinctively touched the sword at his side, and he thought about the three heirloom grenades he had clipped to his belt. He lowered the spyglass and returned it to its pocket. His best chance was to sneak in under cover of darkness. It would make finding a power cell more difficult, but hopefully by crossing the plain at night, he would not alert the tokmen to his presence.

He shuffled back from the edge of the escarpment, and checked his surroundings once more. He listened to the air for any sign of danger. Then he unshouldered his light pack and sat in the dirt. He satiated his hunger with a piece of dried ubok and settled in to watch the fall of night.

He was alone now, well and truly alone. He was still young, twenty winters this past year, and yet all his life he had fought with death. When he had been eight, his father, Mathar, died on an expedition to the east. Before he died, they said, he had fought off ten Taivars singlehandedly so his companions could escape. Four years later Rithik's sister, Praya, died of winter sickness. His mother survived, but had died inwardly after setting Praya's body out in the wilderness. She hadn't even said goodbye when Rithik left Tavala, as all those infected with ghost flesh must.

The red sun grew wide and hit the horizon like a fireball, spreading its weird orange light across the western sky. In the east, the gathering darkness already chased the light across the heavens. Rithik leaned back and watched the stars come out, and the deep blue of twilight turn to black of night.

Lights out, he thought. That was death, the approach of a starless night, a darkness so deep no thought could hold it, no dream could appear in it. That was what happened to the ancients. Death had come for them all.

Even they could not stop it, whose great civilization had spread across the world, whose power had reached out to the heavens themselves. Now all that was left were ghosts, and the ruins of their empty cities.

Almost empty, he thought, remembering the tokmen. He gathered his things and rose to his feet. He shouldered his pack, brushed the dirt from his clothes, and made his way down around the back of the escarpment. As a hunter he had long grown accustomed to traveling by little more than starlight. If he hurried, he would make it to the city before moonrise, with less chance of being seen by tokmen. At the bottom, he set out across the plain, toward the city of dust, and whatever end fate would grant him.

2

CITY OF DUST

The people of Tavala had always been champions of hope. Hope kept them going. Hope was what made life worth living on the edge of the wastelands. They hoped the next harvest would bring more food. They hoped raiders would not return from the north. They hoped some discovery in the ruins would make life easier for them and their children. They did not yet dare to hope for a return to the glory of the ancients, and yet they always hoped for something more.

With the ghost flesh lodged inside him, Rithik didn't know what he was hoping for anymore. And yet he hoped, perhaps out of sheer force of habit, as he trod across the darkness of the barren plain. He hoped not to be spotted by the tokmen. He hoped to find a power cell for his torch among the ruins. He hoped … that was enough for now. He could make out the edges of the ruins in the darkness.

The high towers loomed ahead, blotting out the stars in the black of a still moonless sky.

He stopped for a moment, listened for any sound that carried on the night air, scanned the edges of his vision for any sign of movement. All was quiet. Maybe the tokmen had moved on or died off. Maybe they had all killed each other, and left the city of dust for him to plunder. He could only hope.

He moved with the stealth of a hunter, his leather boots padding softly on the hard ground. But as he entered the ruins of the outer city, he felt less like a predator, and more like prey.

The faint traces of ancient roads, which had been visible from the top of the escarpment, became apparent on the ground only as ruined buildings began to line the roads that led toward the center of the city. The crumbled facades and ancient torch poles, which had long ago gone out, already towered above him. Rithik pulled his filter mask up and over his nose and mouth. He hugged the edges of the building on one side, well aware of how exposed and vulnerable he was. No hunters had risked an expedition into the city of dust for over a generation. Yet here he was, alone, with little else but his questionable wits and his sword.

Most of the doorways were almost completely buried in the ghost-filled sand that had blown in from the desert beyond. But every window, every gap in the crumbled walls contained a darkness that seemed blacker than black. Tokmen could be lurking in any one of these buildings and he would never know until they attacked. The outer reaches had likely been looted in times long past, and since he aimed for the desert beyond, he headed straight toward the center of the city.

As he went, he found himself wondering if it wouldn't have been wiser to have waited in the wilderness for death. There at least a lion might find him, instead of the tokmen. But he could no more give up than he could forsake his own name, or forget that he was … or at least had been, a hunter of Tavala.

The farther he went, the higher the buildings became, until their summits could no longer be made out against the darkness of the night sky. He walked silently on, by the faint glimmer of starlight, through long canyons of hollowed out ceramite. The smooth ceramic-like material was harder than steel and more resilient. But nothing lasts forever. The rounded, organic shapes of the ancient towers were pockmarked and chipped into ruins by the ravages of time.

Here and there, the deteriorating hulks of former conveyances stuck out of the sand, half buried. Flitter cars, the hunters had called them, in which the ancients once sped along their roads, and through the air as well, if the stories were to be believed. Some said the ancients had walked on the moon and beyond, even traveled to the stars. Some said they had controlled the very atoms of matter, and even the forms of life. While that may have been so, Rithik thought, what good had it done them? They were all long gone.

A sound startled him. He ducked his head and dashed through a nearby window. Whirling around, he hid himself behind the ceramite wall, and peered out. Across the street some debris fell from high above. It clattered against the building as it dropped, landing with a series of soft thuds in the deep dust and sand that covered the road. Probably just weathering, he thought, but nevertheless he stood silent and motionless for several minutes, listening for any further sound or signs of movement.

Satisfied, he turned toward the interior of the building. Now that he was inside, he might as well look around and start his search for a power cell. It was pitch black inside. He moved deeper in, away from the windows, and took a glowjar from one of his vest pockets. Inside was a handful of luminescent aquatic mushrooms floating in fresh water. He shook the jar and their faint bluish glow intensified. Soon they produced enough light to see about ten feet around him.

The floor was buried in a thick layer of sand and dust. He turned the volume down on his chatter box, then crouched down and risked turning it on. A near constant crackling chatter emitted from the box, and he switched it off again. The place was crawling with ghosts.

In the scant light of the glowjar, he could see the ceiling had collapsed in the middle of the large room he found himself in. Peering up through the hole was pointless though. He could make out nothing but darkness above. In places, counters and tables jutted out of the sand, lined with dead screens, scraps of ancient paper, jot sticks, and other pieces of junk.

He scanned the artifacts, picking up and discarding a few odd items. He was looking for certain portable devices he knew would contain a standard power cell. He saw nothing promising though, and moved on. That was the life of a hunter. You had to be pretty lucky to find what you were looking for straight off.

Deeper in, he found some rooms as yet unburied in sand. He came across several portable screens that looked promising, but they wouldn't power up, and one by one he tossed them aside. He went clear through the building, pausing once to pry open an empty closet, once to investigate some plastic crates, and once to take a leak in the corner.

He exited through a window in the bare ceramite hull on the far side of the building. To his left and right stretched a long, wide avenue lined with high towers. A broken moon was rising, casting a cold, muted light down the length of the avenue. He concealed the glowjar, turned left, and headed deeper into the center of the city. After some time, he ventured into another building. He was guided by instinct … or blind chance. That was always a debate among hunters, but where anyone settled on the matter usually depended on how successful they were.

This was the building, he thought. Somewhere in here he would find his power cell. He brought out his glowjar and began his search. The bottom floor was mostly barren though, and he felt the pangs of disappointment as he searched through room after room. Eventually he found a half-open door leading to a column of stairs, and he ventured up. The higher one went, they said, the greater the treasures. Sometimes it was even true.

The second level door was shut tight and wouldn't budge. The third level door was stuck, but moved a few inches when Rithik pushed on it. He pushed with more and more of his weight. It felt like it would give way, if he just put a little more into it. He stepped back and shouldered into the door with all his might. With a crash it gave way and Rithik tumbled inward onto the ground.

He landed on his side, face to face with a withered corpse. He stared into its gaping eye sockets. He started for a moment, scrambling back, but just as quickly calmed himself. He rolled up into a half crouch, resting on one knee, and held out his glowjar to examine the body. Dried skin was stretched tight across the skull. The flesh around the mouth had receded, revealing two rows of crooked, rotting, and missing teeth. It was dressed in tattered rags.

This was no ancient one. This was a modern human being. A tokman? Or a hunter who had met his fate? He glanced back at the door. It had been barricaded with a large cabinet. He glanced around the room. There were signs of a small fire nearby, some discarded food containers, a ceramite-tipped spear. He looked desperately for any sign of something that might have a power cell. Finding nothing, he glanced back at the dead body. That would be him if he tarried in this city too long.

No sooner had he thought it than a deep, horrifying scream broke the silence of the building, echoing up through its hollow chambers. It was a terror-filled sound, a kind of blood curdling battle cry that sent a chill up his spine and made the skin on the back of his head twitch and tighten. Other screams immediately followed, unintelligible shouts, rattles, and the frantic, arrhythmic beating of a drum.

Tokmen!

3

THE TOKMEN

Rithik drew his razor-sharp ceramite sword and dashed back to the door. He poked his head out into the column of stairs that wound their way up through the interior of the tower. He heard the shouts of the tokmen on the levels below. There were a lot of them, and it sounded like they were looking for something. He could only assume it was him. Going down that way wasn't a good idea, but he didn't like the idea of barricading himself in either. It obviously hadn't been a good plan for the former resident.

He took a chance and went up, bounding up the stairs as quickly and as quietly as he could. At the very least it might buy him some time while they searched the lower levels. With that thought, he flew past levels four and five. By level six he started to wonder how he would get down, so he darted through an open doorway. He paused in a large open area with countertops, tables, and the skeletons of once-padded chairs.

One part of his mind, ever the hunter, was still looking for something that might hold a standard power cell. But he could hear the grunts, snorts, and squeals of the tokmen as they came up the stairs. So another part of his mind just said *run*, and was looking for nothing other than an escape route. That part of his mind was quickly taking over.

Hiding was out of the question. No matter how well you hid, success or failure always depended on how thoroughly somebody looked for you. At least if he kept moving he had a fighting chance. He found a room full of lift chutes, but even if he found a clear one, that was just a more difficult way down to where the tokmen were waiting.

He ran down a hallway and into a room with a long bank of windows. Desperate, he stuck his head out and peered down through the darkness. It took only a glance to figure a fall from this height was certain death, if not from impact, then from the crowds of tokmen gathered in the street below. They looked mostly human … but even at this distance, their movement was unsettling, a kind of jerky shambling that seemed neither human nor animal, but something else entirely.

As he stood looking out the window, he could hear the tokmen in the building getting closer. There was nowhere to go. But just as he started to think hiding might be his only chance, he noticed a sky tunnel bridging this level with the building across the street. The entrance couldn't be far off.

He ran out of the room, opting for maximum speed over any semblance of stealth. Down a hall he went, bashed open a door, then another one, but no sky tunnel. It had to be close. He ran back out into the corridor, heard a horrible squeal behind him, and glanced back the way he had come. A horde of misshapen man-things, wrapped in skins, hurried toward him. One had no jaw. One had three eyes. And one had a face that seemed nothing but teeth, gnashing away as it came for him. Old bones hung off of them, and they carried nail-studded clubs and long scrap-metal knives.

Rithik turned and ran down the hallway into a wide open space. The tokmen came after him, but the sky tunnel was just ahead. A wide portal and a long passage led through the air toward the other building. With the tokmen close behind, the darkness on the other side beckoned him forward.

He dashed into the tunnel and ran across. At one time the walls of the tunnel must have mostly been glass. Enough of it was gone now that the wind blew through, and it felt as if he was running through the air, high above the earth. He heard the screeches and grunts of the tokmen, but he just kept running.

Without breaking his stride, he leapt over a four-foot gap in the floor, and only paused to look back when he'd reached the building on the far side. The tokmen were still coming, halfway across the sky tunnel.

Rithik pulled one of the grenades from his belt. He pulled the pin, released the lever, and threw it back down the sky tunnel corridor. One of the tokmen shrieked. Rithik turned away as the grenade went off and a deafening explosion rocked the corridor. He glanced back to see the tokmen were gone and the middle of the tunnel had collapsed. A cloud of dust and debris fell into the street below.

That wasn't the end of his troubles though. Blowing things up was only a temporary solution to any really big problem, and there were still plenty of tokmen out there, maybe a lot more than he cared to imagine. Power cell or no power cell, he needed to get out of this city.

A quick search of the level yielded no sign of stairs. He pried open the doors of a lift chute and climbed down into a deepening darkness on a rickety ladder. He counted levels in the dim light of his glowjar as he descended past each doorway. He found the ground floor doorway already pried open, hopefully long ago, and he stepped out onto the solid floor.

He paused, and hearing no sign of the tokmen, headed—as best as he could tell—away from the other building. This level was a maze of corridors and locked doors. He finally reached what looked like a door outside and threw himself against it with careless abandon.

The door flew open, and he stumbled out into the dusty street. At once he knew he had made a mistake. To his right a big dog stood poised to attack. Its brownish-gray fur twitched over bulging muscles in the moonlight. Short ears flopped to the sides of a broad head. Its beady eyes glared straight ahead, snout jutting out, lips pulled back, and teeth bared in a hideous growl. To his left, three tokmen advanced on him. One had a club, another a spear. The biggest one carried a long pole, tipped with a short, battle-scarred ceramite blade. He had the face of a human skull tied onto his head like a mask.

The tokmen charged. There was no escape. This is just another way to die, Rithik thought, and moved forward to meet them with his sword. Skull face screamed and thrust at Rithik with his ceramite polearm. Rithik dodged, spun forward and cut one of the others in the throat as he raised his club to attack.

The spearman shrieked, turned, and thrust the jagged metal tip of the spear at Rithik's midsection. Sidestepping, Rithik cut down and clear through the spear's shaft. Then he turned the tip of his sword on the spearman and stabbed him in the chest.

For a moment the tokman hung on his sword, as heavy as death. Rithik jerked the sword from the tokman's body, but it was a moment too late. Skull face smashed into him, polearm crosswise, pinning Rithik's sword arm and nearly knocking him off his feet. Rithik scrambled backward to stay upright. He slammed against the building, back pinned to the wall. The tokman was incredibly strong. Beneath the skull-faced mask his jaws opened, revealing rows of sharpened teeth. He leaned in to bite Rithik's neck.

Rithik struggled to reach the knife at his belt with his left hand.

Out of the darkness, the dog leaped onto the tokman. The tokman reeled sideways and the dog brought him down, snapping and biting anything and everything, until he got at his neck. Then his jaws sunk in and didn't let go until the body of the tokman slumped in death.

Rithik held his ground, sword ready, when the dog looked up at him. The dog's bloody face relaxed, and Rithik wasn't sure if it was really a dog now. There was something in its expression that spoke of a creature who had evolved from a dog, but was not entirely a dog anymore. Then its mouth opened and words came out, intelligible words!

"More will come," the dog-creature said in a deep voice, lips shaping the words in a most un-doglike way. "We must go now."

Rithik lowered his sword. "Which way to the desert?"

"Dhis way," the dog said, motioning with his head away down the street. "Follow me." Some of the sounds were muddled in the dog's mouth, but the meaning was clear enough.

Rithik nodded, and the dog went off down the street.

Rithik started after him, but as he passed the dead skull-faced tokman, the glint of something shiny caught his eye. "Wait," Rithik called, and the dog stopped, looking back.

Rithik knelt down by the skull-faced corpse. A battered mini-screen hung from a cord around the tokman's neck. When he reached out and touched the screen, an image of the skull-faced tokman appeared on it and screamed.

Rithik jumped back, stopped himself, then noticed the screen was at three quarters power. He would have bet gold it ran on a standard power cell. He flicked the little screen off, looped the tip of his sword around the leather cord and cut it.

"Hurry!" the dog said.

Rithik slipped the screen into one of his pockets and ran after the talking dog, off into the night, under the cold glare of a broken moon, beneath the crumbling, ancient towers in the long fallen city of dust.

4

THE NIGHT SKY

Rithik had been in a few scraps with raiders and bunyaps. In each case he had managed to survive, but it had been a terrifying, desperate ordeal to the end. He had never fought as he had against those tokmen, with no trace of hesitation. It was as if, having accepted his death in that moment, he had glimpsed some new dimension of being and action. Still he might have died had it not been for the dog, who now trotted ahead of him through the western outskirts of the city. The tokmen had not followed, but that fearless dimension seemed to collapse around him, and the tyranny of death took hold once more in his thoughts.

As for a talking dog, such things were not entirely unheard of. Sharo said once he had a long conversation with a talking badger in the wilderness. Of course he probably had drunk a mugful of karo tea prior to the conversation. On the other hand, the bunyaps certainly had their own language, though few could understand it. And some dogs were said to understand many words. But a dog who could speak the old tongue was somewhat of a novelty.

Presently, the dog zig-zagged his way up the slope of a moonlit sand dune. The desert had all but completely buried the ruins on this western edge of the city. Rithik climbed the dune. The sand gave way beneath his feet with each step, and he slid back half a step for each step he took. By the time he reached the top, his chest heaved as he breathed through the filter mask.

He followed the dog's gaze westward. Before them stretched a seemingly endless sea of sand, with dune-waves frozen in the pale glow of the broken moon.

"Dhere," the dog said, as if pointing with his snout. "Desert."

Rithik pulled his filter mask down around his neck. "Thank you."

The big dog looked up at him. "What now?"

"I continue westward," Rithik said. "I suppose we'll part ways here."

"No," the dog said. "I go with you."

Rithik looked out across the dune sea. "That's not a good idea. I am likely going to my death."

"We are all going to our death," the dog said. "Where else would we be going?"

Rithik felt a pang of sadness at the thought. "Some of us may be going sooner than others," he said.

"Don't worry," the dog said. "I can lead dhe way, if you wish."

Rithik almost laughed. "You don't understand." He pulled back the sleeve of his left arm to reveal the purple infection creeping past his elbow, wrapping its tendrils around his bicep. "See. I have the ghost flesh. It is certain death."

"Ghosts cannot harm you," the dog said.

Rithik laughed. "Nevertheless," he said, "I'm going on into the desert. Do not follow me if you treasure your life."

He pulled his filter mask up around his nose and mouth, and started down the gentle west-facing slope. The sand gave way beneath his feet once more, and each step was part footfall, part slide.

After a hundred feet or so he looked back. The dog had descended the summit of the dune and was now following him at a distance.

"Go back," Rithik yelled, his voice muffled by the filter mask. "Go back!"

The dog stopped, but made no move to turn around.

"Go back!" Rithik yelled once more. Then he continued on. He hadn't the energy to worry about what the dog would do. He had his own destiny to think about. And as he walked westward in the moonlight, under the twinkling of distant stars, those signal posts of far-off worlds, his thoughts came flooding in.

What would happen to him when the ghost flesh took hold of his heart or his brain? Would he simply cease to be? Would the beauty of this night sky never come again for him? Would this world of fleeting joy and misery vanish before his eyes? Would these thoughts just stop and never start up again? Would his memories be lost forever? When the goddess Yananna washed his soul of world corruption, would anything remain to be reborn?

Hours passed as he walked due west. His thoughts went round and round, calling up memories of those who had gone before him, and of those who remained in Tavala. He recalled the empty faces he had seen in death. And he regretted not marrying Elaya when he had the chance. But then it was better this way. After all, she had Tavik now and two children, and Rithik had the ghost flesh. All that was over now. He had gone beyond the pale. There was nothing now but this moment, this desert, this starry sky. And he knew not what would happen tomorrow, or in the very next minute, let alone at the hour of his death.

At long last, exhausted and weary of his thoughts, he stopped to rest and drink water. Maybe he could get a few hours sleep before sunrise. He sat cross-legged in the sand right in the spot where he stopped walking. The air was still, but cold. He flicked the chatter box on, and it emitted a non-stop crackling static. He turned it off and adjusted his filter mask.

From one of his pockets he took his glowjar and shook it. The aquatic mushrooms inside lit up with a bluish glow. He noted that it wasn't quite as bright as it had been a few nights ago. He set it down in the sand, got out the other one, shook it, and set it in the sand too. He now sat cross-legged in a circle of bluish light.

In front of him he unrolled a two-foot square of plastic on which he placed a few tools, his dead torch, and the mini-screen he'd taken from the skull-faced tokman.

He heard something in the darkness, and reaching for his sword he rolled up to one knee. But as the first inch of ceramite blade cleared its sheath, he saw the nose of the big dog at the edge of the bluish light. He pushed the sword back into its scabbard, sat once more, and turned his attention to his things.

The dog took a few wary steps into the light and lay down in the sand a few feet from him.

Rithik picked up the mini-screen and activated it. The skull-face tokman appeared and screamed as if he were charging into battle.

The dog leapt to his feet, snapped his jaws twice and growled, baring his teeth.

"It's okay," Rithik said, deactivating the screen and flipping it over to examine the back.

The dog's face softened once more, and his lips moved to speak. "What is dhat?" the dog said.

"A mini-screen," Rithik said. "The magic of the ancients was mediated through screens."

The dog took a step closer and looked at the screen. "Dhe ancients are gone. What use is dheir magic?"

Rithik took a torque-driver and popped open the back of the mini-screen. He removed a slender chip, one by two inches long and almost as thick as the mini-screen. "Standard power cell," he said, holding it up between his thumb and forefinger.

The dog lay back down in the sand without further comment.

Rithik's torch was a cylinder about six inches long, with a translucent tip. Like Rithik, it had seen better days. The casing was battered and scratched from years of use. He opened the bottom and fitted the power cell into an empty slot. Then he sealed it back up and pressed a button on the side. Immediately the torch glowed with a warm yellowish light.

The dog made a sound, a kind of curious "hmm," and lifted his head from the sand.

Rithik ran his finger up a slide panel and the torch shone brighter, until it lit up a large section of the desert around them. Satisfied, he turned it off and returned it to a mesh pocket on his vest. He gathered up his tools, rolled them up in the plastic, and returned them to another pocket.

Then he turned his attention to the dog. "Why did you follow me?"

"Just a feeling I had," the dog said.

"Do you still have that feeling?"

The dog tilted its head a little to the left and studied Rithik. "Yes," he said.

"Well I hope you don't expect a happy end to this journey."

"I expect nothing."

Rithik laughed, but it was a laugh tinged with the fear of his own expectations. The truth was, he had based his plan on the tale of a raving madman. A Yinith trader once told of a rocky oasis due west of the city. He said he had entered the spirit realm and seen the mouth of Yananna's cave, a huge yawning entrance to the underworld. The trader had spent his last days in Tavala though, chewing on nava root and raving like a lunatic. Maybe there really was nothing out there.

The dog curled itself up in the ghost-ridden sand.

"Do you have a name, dog?"

"Once called Waro."

"I'm Rithik." His voice sounded hollow when he said it, as if he was a ghost himself.

"Rest now," Waro said. "Dawn is coming."

5

THE WESTERN DESERT

The sun rose like a vengeful demon, its rays beating down unfiltered by any shred of clouds. The temperature rose quickly, and the fleeting half dreams of fitful slumber faded into the harsh reality of the Western Desert. Rithik sat up and blinked. The dog, Waro, was already awake and staring hard at the western horizon.

Rithik got out some dried ubok and his water bottle. He offered some to Waro, pouring the water in a bowl from his pack. The dog ate and drank without comment. The supply would run out sooner, of course, but a hunter always shared with his companions. There was no other way. He felt a little refreshed after taking some himself, and they started westward with few words and little ceremony.

In their brief bouts of conversation as they traveled west across the barren desert, Rithik learned a little more about his companion. Waro was a wanderer who had traveled down from the north. He had learned the old tongue from Neran tribesmen who took him in when he was young. He knew of no others of his kind, and had wandered through the wastelands for untold years. He had been passing through the city of dust when the tokmen set out to make a meal of him.

The flat horizon stretched in an enormous circle around them. Endless dunes filled the space between them and the edges of that circle. And the sky, cloudless, burning blue, arced above them, an enormous dome, like a heavy lid upon the world. Such vast, open space never felt so small to Rithik. There was no way out. And he felt as trapped by this world around him as he did by the tingling infection that slowly crept up his arm.

He was suddenly grateful that Waro was with him. Nothing stirred in this wasteland but a man and a dog, and the sand beneath their feet. Rithik had seen no animal or plant, not so much as an insect or a blade of dry grass. They could have been on the surface of the moon, or on the desolate plains of an uninhabitable planet.

Rithik wiped sweat from his brow and squinted at the western horizon, which seemed to blur in a kind of haze that merged land and sky. They had walked for hours, stopping only occasionally to drink, but already their water supply was running low. If there was a rocky oasis to the west, it had better be close, or they would die of thirst long before the ghost flesh ran its course.

Waro made a whining, pure dog sound.

Rithik stopped. He crouched down, got out his water bottle, and shook it. The hollow sloshing began to sound as much like doom as relief. "We'll save this," Rithik said.

"Does no good in the bottle," Waro said.

"I've got something else," Rithik said. He got the bowl out of his pack and put it in the sand in front of Waro. Then he took one of the glowjars from his vest pocket. He shook it a little, but the aquatic mushrooms inside had either stopped glowing, or glowed so dimly it wasn't visible in the bright light of day. They would be dead soon anyway, and with his torch working now he had plenty of light. He opened the jar and poured the water and mushrooms into the bowl for Waro.

Waro looked down at the strange looking mushrooms, and then up at Rithik, as if to ask if this was some kind of trick.

Rithik pulled down his filter mask. "They're not bad," he said. He got out the other jar, opened it, and drank the water. Then he shook the mushrooms into his mouth. The bland rubbery mushroom flesh oozed moisture as he chewed them.

Waro lapped up the water and mushrooms in a matter of seconds, and licked the bowl until there was nothing left.

Rithik gazed westward once more. The haze on the horizon had grown. Land and sky were now indistinguishable. "We better keep moving," he said, putting the bowl and the empty jars in his pack.

They continued on, saying nothing of the haze ahead. Time seemed to slow, measured only by their footfalls in the sand. The dusty haze grew to fill the whole western sky, and still they said nothing, until the wind picked up, blowing out of the west.

"A storm's coming," Rithik said.

"For some time now," Waro said.

"Nothing to do but keep going."

Waro just barked. It was pure canine, but somehow clear in its affirmation.

They leaned into the wind, and soon the sand started to blow. The first few particles felt like needles against Rithik's exposed flesh. He pulled his scarf up around his head, adjusted his filter mask, hid his hands in his pockets, and looked down at his feet. He hoped Waro's fur was enough to protect him.

The wind howled, then roared, and when it seemed it could be no louder, it began to come into his mind, such that not even a thought could stand against it.

Visibility went from bad to non-existent in a matter of seconds.

The sand beneath their feet gave way.

They were barely moving.

Sand began to tear at Rithik's clothes.

Every step drove him deeper into exhaustion. Nobody could fight such a storm.

He could barely see Waro at his side.

"We have to stop," Rithik yelled. He was screaming over the sound of the howling wind, but he didn't know if Waro could hear him. He dropped to his knees. He couldn't go another step. "Waro!"

Waro stopped.

Rithik lay down on the blowing sands. He curled up in a ball and turned his back to the wind. He motioned for Waro, and the dog curled up in front of him.

There was nothing to do but wait. In the face of such unrestrained energy, surrender was the only option, and the only chance for survival, however slim.

He shut his eyes tight and felt the sand pile up against his back. For some reason he thought of the first time his father had taken him into the ruins of the river city. He had told Rithik about the ancients, their great power, and their mysterious destruction. He taught Rithik about the dangers of the ruins, what things to look for, and the best places to look.

Since then, he had been a hunter of Tavala, but all that had ended. He was a wanderer now, like Waro, and maybe that would end soon too. The wind howled. He could feel the sand heavy on his side and piled high against his back. They would be buried soon. Maybe this was it then. What could he say, even if Waro could hear him? Perhaps sorry … perhaps thanks … perhaps …

6

ENTRANCE TO THE UNDERWORLD

A giant majestic bird soared overhead in a clear blue sky. Wings outstretched, it circled round and round. Then it passed in front of the blinding sun and swooped down at Rithik. Its great talons grabbed hold of his body and lifted him up into the air. He felt the huge wings beat above him. His head lolled sideways and he watched the desert ground recede away beneath them. Higher and higher they went, until the endless dunes seemed a mere abstraction. But when he turned his head to look in the direction they flew, he saw a long outcropping of rock stretched across the horizon.

The rocky outcrop got nearer and nearer, rising up like an island in the sea of sand. When they reached it, the great bird circled round once more. Rithik could see a long deep fissure in the rock below. There were green trees down there, and a shimmering pool of water. And there, on the far side of the pool, was a gaping hole, a huge yawning cave.

Suddenly, the bird folded its wings back and dove straight at the cave entrance. Faster and faster they went. The wind rushed by, and the great black hole of the cave got larger and larger, until it filled Rithik's vision. They flew right into it, into a darkness darker than anything Rithik had ever known, into a void so empty it could hold no thought, no memory, no dream.

If this was death, Rithik thought, it felt a lot like waking up after dozing off unexpectedly. His neck was sore, and his breath shallow. When he opened his eyes it was still dark. But he felt alive, and strangely he realized this was the only indicator one could ever have. He could feel the weight of sand on top of him, but something was different.

Silence, that's what it was. The howl of the wind was gone.

He moved a leg, then an arm, wiggling it back and forth beneath the sand. He felt a scrambling of movement next to him. A moment later he heard Waro barking. He felt the dog tugging at his sleeve, then digging in the sand around him.

Rithik pulled at the sand with his other hand, shook his head, his shoulders, and finally moved forward, clawing his way out of the dune in which he was buried.

Waro tugged at his sleeve one last time, then backed up, barked, and turned around in a circle.

Rithik sat up, adjusted his filter mask, and shook as much sand off himself as he could. It took a moment to realize it was night. The broken moon was setting and the clear sky was filled with stars.

"I had a dream," Rithik said, "that the great eagle Samsa carried me away to the west."

Waro looked west, then back to Rithik. "No eagle will carry us," he said. "We must walk."

They drank what was left of Rithik's water. Within moments a glow appeared on the eastern horizon, and they set off in the opposite direction. After some time, the sun rose, and they saw in the west an outcropping of rock.

Rithik stopped. "It is just as I saw in my dream."

"What else was in dhis dream?"

"Water … and the entrance to Yananna's cave."

"Who is Yananna?"

"A goddess of the underworld, where the dead are cleansed and prepared for rebirth."

Waro looked at him as if his words meant nothing. "Water is good," he said.

With a goal in sight Rithik felt a surge of energy, and they marched forward at nearly twice their former pace. Still, it took them half the morning to reach the rocks, and not a moment too soon. Rithik's mouth felt as dry as the sand by the time they stepped onto solid ground.

They climbed up the gentle rise and there, at the top, looked down into the gorge Rithik had seen in his dream. It was just as it had been. He could feel the moisture even here at the edge. Green trees grew from ledges and cracks in the steep walls of the gorge. Below, a pool of water shimmered in the midday sun. In the rock wall beyond the pool was the entrance to a cave.

"Water!" Waro said.

"Yananna's cave," Rithik said.

"Water first."

"Let's go."

They found a way down the steep gorge, switched back several times, doubled back once, and finally made it to the bottom.

Tiny lizards dashed out of the way as Waro bounded forward and leapt into the water. He splashed around, shook himself, turned around in a circle, and finally bent his head down to drink.

Rithik approached slowly, his eyes fixed in awe on the yawning cave entrance beyond the pool. That must be it, he thought, just as the old man had said. Were they in the spirit realm now, then, he wondered. When had they crossed over?

"Water," Waro said, and dipped his head back down to drink more.

Would one need water in the spirit realm? Although he had dreamed of this place, Rithik was no dream dweller.

He knew little of such things, but there was no doubt he was thirsty. He dropped to his knees at the edge of the pool, flicked on the chatter box and ran it over the surface of the water. It emitted a slow crackling stream of noise, but the levels were safe enough. Not that it mattered. Ghosts or no ghosts he was going to drink.

He filled his bottle, then poured the sweet tasting water into his mouth and swallowed. He drank until he couldn't drink any more. Then he filled up all his empty containers. He washed the grime from his hands and pulled up his left sleeve. He couldn't see the ghost flesh moving, but he knew it was. The purplish tendrils reached farther than they had a few days ago.

The yawning cave entrance beckoned him. He remembered his dream and the unfathomable darkness within. He felt lost staring into that darkness. He felt desperate, and he had nothing to lose.

Waro sat beside him and followed his gaze toward the cave entrance. "What do you expect to find in dhere?"

Rithik stared into the darkness, but no amount of staring would reveal anything. "Maybe life," he said. "Maybe death."

"You can find dhat anywhere," Waro said.

Rithik turned to look at his canine friend. "I don't expect you to go with me." He began to gather up his things. He took half his supply of dried ubok and left it on the rocks. "If you continue west, you should make it to

Rualatin. There's a settlement there that might welcome you."

Waro said nothing.

Rithik shouldered his small pack. He had to go now while his resolve was still with him. "So long," he said, and started to make his way around the pool.

"Wait," Waro said.

Rithik couldn't wait. He had come to find Yananna's cave, and if this was it, to find the goddess herself before death took him. That is why he had risked entering the city of dust. That is why he had crossed the Western Desert. That was all he had left. He had to know what was inside. He had to keep looking.

He climbed up onto a ledge that led to the cave's entrance. He could hear Waro on the rocks behind him, but he didn't look back. He stood now in front of the cave entrance. From here, light penetrated inward far enough to see into a chamber vaulted in natural stone.

Rithik walked a few feet in. The floor of the chamber sloped downward to where, near the middle of the room, a fissure in the rock appeared to lead down into the depths of the cave.

Waro stood at the entrance now. "Why not rest first?"

"There's no time," Rithik said, and he climbed down into the darkness.

7

FLOWERS OF DARKNESS

Rithik made his way down a near vertical passage from the chamber above. Finally he dropped through several feet of empty space to land on level ground.

The darkness was almost complete. Looking up, he could still see a faint trace of light filtering down from the chamber above. He saw no sign of Waro. He half hoped the dog would follow him, half hoped he would make it to Rualatin.

He reached into his pocket, took out his torch and turned it on. The light filled the chamber, shining out in every direction from the translucent end cap. The floor here was lined with sediment and scattered with small rocks, as if a stream had flowed through at some point. The walls were bare stone. A distant trickle of water echoed out of the darkness, but beyond that was silence—deep, ancient silence. Behind him the chamber was closed off, but ahead a tunnel large enough to walk through led deeper.

To free up his hands, Rithik returned the torch to its pocket, where the light shone clearly through the mesh. He moved forward into the tunnel. The truth was, he didn't know what to expect. Even if this was Yananna's cave, the old trader had not ventured inside, and no legend told what lay within, nor dared to describe the goddess. "What words could touch a goddess?" Sharo would say. "What vision can conjure the end of all things?"

Rithik knew not, so he moved ahead with equal measures of caution and curiosity.

Traces of spindly root-like growths clung to the walls. As he went deeper into the tunnel, they grew into a labyrinthine network of structures that covered every surface of the stone. He had never seen anything like it.

The darkness of the tunnel unfolded before his advancing light. To the left and right, more tunnels branched off, but he continued straight. Farther in, he saw strange plant things growing out of the network of roots. Each one was a few feet across, with four white leathery leaves spreading out from a central node.

As he passed, stalks emerged from the nodes and bloomed into strange vermillion flowers. They seemed to greet him, and led him deeper and deeper down the long passage. A sweet, spicy aroma filled the air. The smell was not something he could place, but it was pleasant, and vaguely familiar, as if touching some distant trace of memory he could not quite grasp.

He stopped to examine one of the flowers more closely. The petals had an iridescent sheen to them. He leaned in close and inhaled. When he did the center of the flower opened up and disgorged a cloud of powdery white pollen.

Startled, Rithik stepped back. The floral aroma overwhelmed his senses. His legs swayed on the uneven ground. He heard the echoes of his footsteps long after he made them. He turned to look down the passage, and perceived a strange warping of his view. Things far seemed near, and things near seemed distorted, small. His mind swam through a parade of sensations.

Thoughts rose like luminescent bubbles from the dark pool of consciousness, like the pixilated lights on an old screen. He was aware the pollen had affected him, had transformed his awareness, as Kava tea did for dream dwellers. But he was all caught up in it. He could do nothing but watch. Thoughts came and went, but he could not hold them. And that smell … that smell was like … was like a lost love he had never fully realized.

The network of roots appeared to move, creeping ever into unseen distances. Already he felt disoriented, and could not remember which way he had come from. He turned one way and then another, but could not remember.

Then, at the edge of his light he saw a woman dressed in white. It was Elaya, her hair flowing free of braids, as she had worn it on her wedding day. She looked at him, seemed about to say something, then turned down a side passage.

That's it, Rithik thought. That smell … it was Elaya. How could he have forgotten that smell? If only he could tell her how he felt about her.

He stumbled ahead, turning down the side passage to find her. If only he could tell her he still wanted to be with her, that he would never love another as he loved her.

Passing another tunnel, the smell was even stronger, and he turned again. At the next intersection, he looked left and saw a touch of white at the edge of his torch light. He followed it.

Rithik laughed. She was playing a game with him, teasing him, as she had done when she left the bonfire at his sixteenth mid-summer festival. Suddenly he felt just as he had on that night, filled with a love he had never experienced, driven by a desire he did not fully understand. And as he ran through the tunnels after her, he saw the trees of the forest south of Tavala.

Elaya ran ahead of him. She glanced back to make sure he was chasing her, and then ran deeper into the forest.

They ran and ran, until they came into a small clearing, lit by a swelling moon.

Elaya stopped in the center of the clearing. She turned and her face beckoned him like the face of a goddess. He had never seen anything so beautiful, so radiant in the moonlight. He burst with an adoration and a longing he could not contain. She welcomed him into her arms. His hands embraced her supple body. At last, they found each other in a kiss, their eyes closed … their hearts open.

He wanted to be there, in that moment, forever and ever. Somehow he knew he wasn't though. He couldn't be. But where was he?

When Rithik came to his senses, the scene around him and all its associated sensations vanished into the darkness of the cave. He found himself in an unfamiliar passageway, suspended in midair by thick vines of plant matter that wrapped him up, arms, legs, and torso. Beneath him, his right foot was held in the mouth-like orifice of a large bulbous white pod.

He felt no immediate pain other than the discomfort of his outstretched limbs. He struggled against the vines, once, twice, pulling each limb in every direction he could, but to no avail. Finally he slumped in his bonds to rest and clear his mind before trying again.

But the vision of Elaya was still with him. His chest tightened in a torrent of emotion. He thought he had let go of her years ago. He thought he had accepted her marriage to Tavik. Not that he knew where he was, but now that he knew he would probably die here, and that he would never see Elaya again, he realized he had never really let go. He had built a dam in his heart to stop the flow of his feelings for her, and as that dam presently broke, he cried and cried. He was ashamed of his tears, but he could not wipe them away. Nothing that ever happened could be wiped away.

8

The Undergrowth

After some time, Rithik lay spent, held in place by the strong vines, his foot apparently being slowly digested by a mutant cave plant. Although he was uncomfortable, so far at least there was no pain. The torch, still in its mesh pocket, illuminated the strange scene for his amusement, or for the amusement of anybody who might happen upon him, though nobody came. He may have dozed off for a while, fading in and out of consciousness in his utter exhaustion.

Then, somewhere in the distance he heard a long low howl. He thought of Waro, but surely the dog had moved on by this time. He had no idea how long he had even been in here. It could have been hours. It could have been all night, here where there was no day or night. Waro could be half way to Rualatin.

He heard the howl again. And two distinct barks, dog barks. It was unmistakable. Could he be dreaming? Hallucinating?

"Howooooooo."

It was Waro, he thought. It had to be Waro.

Rithik took a breath and yelled, "Waro! Waro!"

"Rarf, rarf … hawoooo!"

It had to be him. The damn dog could speak but not yell.

"Waro! Where are you?"

Waro kept howling, but the sound got no closer. He must have been trapped too, somewhere in the maze of tunnels. The thought of Waro bound up in the darkness gave Rithik new strength. He pulled at the vines with all his might. He tugged and yanked to the point where he felt his joints would tear apart before the vines would. All he had gained was a few inches of slack, such that he hung in an even more uncomfortable position.

"Howooo …" Waro's howls grew weaker.

"Hang on, Waro! I'll come get you." But how? How would he free Waro when he couldn't free himself?

He turned one way so he hung almost solely by his right arm. Then he turned the other, leaning sideways so he hung by his left arm and leg. And there, maybe with the additional slack on his right arm, maybe he could reach his sword.

He contorted himself even further, reached across his body with his right arm, and could just grab hold of the pommel of his sword. With a sharp tug he managed to pull the razor-sharp blade a few inches out of the sheath.

"Howo …"

Rithik twisted until the few inches of exposed blade made contact with one of the vines wrapped around his torso. He applied a little pressure, and once the blade broke through the outer layer of the vine, it quickly cut clean through.

He shifted back and forth exploring the new found movement in his torso, and found another vine he could hook and cut with the sword. Then another. And now, by shifting his hips back, he cleared the full ceramite blade from its sheath.

With a flick of the wrist he cut several vines, freeing his sword arm entirely.

There was no time to figure out a graceful way down. He arced the blade downward, slashing through several vincs until his left leg swung free. Then he arced the blade up over his head and fell to the ground. His full weight dropped onto the pod that held his right foot. The thing tightened its grip and Rithik tumbled sideways to the ground. He rolled upright, brought the tip of his sword to bear, and plunged it into the white pod, careful not to stab his own foot.

A white, digestive slime oozed out of the pod. Within seconds he had cut himself free and scrambled to his feet. The leather of his boot was half eaten through, but it was still intact.

"Waro?" he yelled.

Nothing.

"Waro? I'm free! I'm coming to find you, but you gotta howl."

He listened.

The bulbous pod quivered, and three vines reached out for him.

Rithik took a step back and hacked them apart with two quick slices of his sword. Then he lunged forward and stabbed the pod again for good measure.

"Hr … Hr … Howooooo!"

Rithik looked right then left, and ran toward Waro's howl.

Here and there vines reached out for him, and he slashed through them on the run or dashed by, leaping over the gaping mouths of the pods that accompanied them. He stopped at intersections, listening for Waro's next howl, and when he heard it he was off and running again.

The howls were louder and louder now, until he turned a corner and saw the dog suspended by vines in the passage ahead. He was upside down, with all four limbs going in different directions, and his head staring into the gaping mouth of a pod thing below.

"Don't move," Rithik said.

"Is dhat a joke?"

"No." Rithik lunged forward and slashed down diagonally, right past Waro's left ear and clear through the pod below. The remains of its mouth curled back in vegetal agony. With three quick slashes Rithik cut through the vines binding his friend.

The dog tumbled to the ground and rolled onto all fours without missing a beat.

"We have to get away from these plants," Rithik said. "Which way did you come from?"

"Don't know," Waro said. "I followed your scent in the darkness, but something happened … I got lost."

"Me too."

"Pick a direction," Waro said, "and keep turning right."

"Huh?"

"To find your way out of a labyrinth."

Rithik thought a second. "Ah, right."

"Or left," Waro said, "Doesn't matter."

Rithik shook his head. "Just follow me!" And he ran ahead, turning right at the first intersection. He slashed at some vines that reached out for them, and took another right, right, and right again.

As long as they kept running most of the vines reacted too slowly to latch on to them, but there were more and more of them. Another right, and another. The vines grew thicker and thicker, and Rithik started to wonder whether they should have gone left. Maybe it did matter, after all.

It was too late to change directions now, so he just kept turning right. At last they entered a wide corridor interlaced with thick crisscrossing branches. They paused at the entrance, but they couldn't stop long. The vines had filled in the passage behind and were already stretching out toward them.

This better be the way through, Rithik thought, or they were about to charge forward to their doom. If he couldn't hack his way through, there was no place else to go.

"Dhere's no more vines ahead," Waro said. "Just branches. Follow me!"

The dog ran ahead, lowered to a crouch and scooted under the crisscrossing branches.

Rithik, close on his heels, dove in after him. He crawled forward on the hard ground, bashing every inch of his body against the rock, and every inch of his skull against one branch or another. But after twenty feet he wriggled out, rolled down a gentle slope, and came to rest on a surprisingly flat floor.

Wait a minute.

He rolled to his side and up onto one knee. The ceiling was a natural cavern overhead, but the floor was finished with flat concrete.

A dim orange light came on, flanking a wide metal door set into a concrete wall at the far side of the room.

Waro barked once and then was silent.

A soft, disembodied voice echoed through the room. "Welcome to Evacuation Center Five. Remain calm. All evacuees will be processed in the order they arrive."

9

CITY OF DOOM

Rithik approached the big metal door cautiously. His mind worked to find some explanation. It looked like something the ancients would have built.

"What is dhis place?" Waro said.

"I don't know," Rithik said. Why such a thing would be here he could not fathom. If this was Yananna's cave, what was a ruin doing here?

The door was a foot thick of solid silver metal. It had no outside handle, but stood several feet ajar. Through the gap Rithik could only see a bit of concrete floor.

"What does 'evacuation' mean?" Waro said.

Rithik thought back to the books his father had made him study. A hunter had to learn to read the old tongue. Reading had been known to save the lives of more than a few hunters over the years, and to secure more than a few great treasures. Thus Rithik knew quite a few words that were no longer in use. "I think it means to abandon, to empty out, something like that."

Waro sniffed the air. "Smells old."

If this was the spirit world, Rithik thought, he could take nothing for granted. Who knew what would be here, or why it might appear. And if it wasn't, then he may have just made the find of a lifetime. Either way, whether in search of the goddess Yananna, for some answer to the disappearance of the ancients, or for one last great treasure before death, he felt a compulsion to go ever forward.

Rithik took another few steps toward the open door. He could see now, in the radius of his own light, a few feet down a concrete tunnel beyond. "Let's check it out," he said.

Waro advanced to his side, making no objection.

The inside of the tunnel lit up with more orange lights as they advanced. They went fifty feet before encountering another large metal door. This too was half open. On the outside of the door was a metal placard that read, *Evacuation Site Five. Capacity: 200,000.*

"Two hundred thousand!" Rithik said.

"Dhat's a lot," Waro said.

Rithik couldn't tell if the dog was making a statement or asking a question. "Yes," he said. "That's at least twenty times the size of Pithtek. But still, a fraction of the numbers that would have lived in the old cities."

They passed through the second door, beyond which no lights were operable. Rithik turned the power of his torch up, illuminating part of a large room with several rows of long benches and counters running through the middle. Scattered around, and in overturned baskets were the remnants of old clothes, ancient shoes, papers, and minor personal items.

It was very quiet, as if the silence of centuries had gathered here in the darkness, accumulating over all that time.

Waro sniffed at some of the clothes. "Where is everyone? Usually you find skeletons in an untouched place like dhis."

"I don't know," Rithik said.

They advanced across the room in the circle of light cast by Rithik's torch.

Past a central desk littered with dead screens and decomposing papers, a large sign directed traffic deeper into the facility. An arrow pointing left was marked *Quarantine*, to the right *Administration*, straight ahead a long defunct autostair led steeply downward. That way was marked *Habitats*.

The corridor to the left was blocked by a large, seamless metal door covered with prominent warning symbols, blood signs, ghost signs, and another Rithik couldn't identify. The heavy looking door appeared to have dropped into place from the ceiling above.

Rithik flicked on his chatter box and ran it along the edges of the door. A random scattering of clicks and scratches emanated from the speaker. Levels were low, out here anyway. But he knew what quarantine meant, and even if they had a chance of opening this door, which was doubtful, some doors were best left unopened.

"This way," he said, heading down the administration hall. They ventured into a maze of corridors, open doors, and small, mostly identical offices. Everything seemed in disarray, as if the whole complex had been hastily abandoned. A few screens flickered to life when Rithik touched them, running on independent power. He was lost, however, when it came to navigating or interpreting the images and information that appeared on the screens.

With so many rooms, so much to explore, they moved quickly, skipping some rooms and ducking into others. Every darkened hall, each empty room, exuded a silence that spoke more deeply of mystery than any ruin Rithik had been in. What had happened to these people? Where had they gone?

Rithik forced open a jammed door.

Waro barked.

There in the office, a skeleton was seated at the desk, clothed in a dusty, ancient one-piece suit. His head was lolled back and to one side, jaw agape. His dark empty eye sockets gazed perpetually upward. He appeared held together by the barest scraps of mummified flesh.

They entered. Rithik moved around the desk to the left, while Waro trotted around the other side. The screen on the desk was inoperable, but a stack of strange cards were set on the table in front of it. One card had been turned up. It depicted a ghostly armored skeleton bearing a black flag. On the horizon, between two towers, the sun either set or rose. Across the top was printed a word in the old tongue: *Death*.

Rithik thought it best to leave the rest of the cards untouched.

From the side of the corpse, Rithik noticed the man had a hole blown clear through his skull. His right arm dangled. The bony fingers seemed to point at the ground, where a metallic object lay on the floor.

It was a small hand-held bolt gun. He had seen something like it in a book his father once showed him. Supposedly such artifacts had been common in the years that followed the fall of the ancients, but when their ammunition and their charges ran out, they were useless. Some were lost, some were held as relics and ornaments, and others were melted down for the rare alloys they were made of. In Pithtek such raw materials had value. But a working bolt gun was a rare treasure.

Rithik reached down to pick the gun up.

"What is it?" Waro said.

"A weapon. This poor bastard killed himself."

Waro sniffed at the corpse. "I don't like it. Why would he do dhat?"

"I don't know."

Rithik examined the gun. He understood the basic idea. He thumbed a panel on the side. It showed a charge and thirteen bolts ready to fire. He was tempted to test it. Better to save the bolts though, he thought, and slipped it into a pocket.

Rithik searched the desk for any hint of what had happened here, but there was nothing. He looked back at the dead man. In all his years he had never felt closer to the mystery of the ancients. What had happened here? What had happened to them all?

"Let's move on," Waro said. "We should look for food and a place to rest."

Rithik nodded and left the ancient skeleton as they had found him, his empty eyes gazing eternally at a world he had long ago left behind.

They found nothing more in administration. They doubled back to the main entry chamber and started down the long stair to the habitats. Soon the bubble of light from Rithik's torch illuminated little else but darkness above and darkness below.

"Maybe we'll find a way out," Waro said.

"Maybe."

10

DEATH AMONG THE RUINS

The ghost flesh slowly crept up Rithik's arm. It felt like a tingling numbness, like emptiness. He would almost say it felt like nothing, but that didn't make sense because he could feel it. The wisdom of the hunters said there was always another way out. But something else told him there was no other way out. For him, there was no way out. Was it the ghost flesh speaking to him? Was it this place?

He could not help it that Waro had followed him and was lost here too. He knew eventually he might have to leave him, and everything else for that matter. But for the moment he was glad to have company. A dark place is never quite as dark with a friend at one's side. And Waro, he thought, was a good friend.

When they reached the bottom of the long stairs they again entered a large open area, the limits of which could not be seen in the circle of light provided by the torch. This appeared to be the central hub of the habitats, which radiated outward in wide corridors. Around the perimeter of the hub, they found abandoned shops, restaurants, and communal areas. Every place looked abandoned on short notice, with things left out haphazardly or scattered on the floor, as if there had been a great rush to leave.

In the center of the hub was a garden. At least, it appeared to have been a garden at one time. A labyrinth of raised planter beds spiraled inward from the outer promenade, but all that was in them was dirt. A shallow moat ringed the center, half full of murky water. In the center stood the hulking trunk of a dead tree. Its gnarled branches ended in stumps.

Rithik hopped across the moat for a closer look.

Waro barked, and then growled.

Rithik stopped, looked back. "What is it?"

Waro just growled, his gaze focused on the tree.

Rithik followed Waro's eyes.

One of the branches moved!

Rithik stepped back and drew his sword.

Something on the branch slithered sideways, and then dropped to the ground. It was a worm-like thing, about four feet in length. It had a gaping mouth, but no eyes or face to speak of.

Rithik held his sword ready. The thing slithered like a snake across the ground, but it ignored him and slid into the murky water of the moat.

Rithik relaxed. There was life, he thought, even here there was life. And yet ... where had all the people gone?

"Dhis way," Waro said. "Dhere must be better food here dhan dhat."

Although the ovens of the restaurants had long gone cold, they found some canned food of a kind Rithik had never seen, and which hadn't been found for generations on the surface. The food proved good, and they had soon gorged themselves on unheard of delicacies, like *chili* and *tuna*.

After eating their fill, they slept in shifts in the corner of a common area.

Rithik dreamt of his father and the ruins of the river city. He was only a boy when he first ventured with his father into the ruins. His father's weapons and tools jangled at his sides as they walked. Rithik craned his neck at the ceramite towers, which grew taller and taller the farther they ventured into the city.

"Look there," his father said, "an old flitter car."

"What is it?"

"A kind of carriage the ancients used to fly through the air."

"But it has no wings. Birds all have wings. Even bats, flies, and beetles have wings."

"The ancients flew with a power unknown to us. Their magic was deep. Alas, some say it was their ruin. The gods became jealous, and smote them in their days of glory."

Side by side they crossed the south bridge, stopping half way to look down at the river. The water was crystal clear and on the bottom huge chunks of crumbled ceramite lay lodged in the sand.

On the far side, they walked along the ceramite canyons of ancient boulevards.

"Pick one," his father said. "Pick a building."

"That one," Rithik said, pointing at the tallest tower he could see.

They entered through the open front and found a bank of lift chute doors. Rithik's father jammed a rusted crowbar into one of the doors.

"Where did they all go?" Rithik said. "How did they die?"

"Who really knows," his father said, pulling at the crowbar. The door slid open. Inside they found a service ladder. "Now up you go."

They went high that day, perhaps the highest he had ever been.

Rithik stepped out of the chute onto the floor, his father close behind him. Somewhere he could hear the wind howling through the hull of the tower, but the air was still on the landing. The tower swayed gently beneath his feet.

They explored down long hallways, opening doors, his father on the left, him on the right, always searching. In the dream, Rithik wondered about this never ending search. They were always searching for something. What were they looking for? It was something more than treasure, something more than a gadget to make life easier, something more even than the secrets of the ancients.

They searched for something always just beyond their grasp. Why else would they keep searching? But what was it? What kept them venturing ever deeper into the ruins? What could ever satisfy this desire, this hunger he felt? What could ever fill this hole in his heart?

His father was searching through a closet in one of the rooms.

Rithik stood in the hall, looking in. "Find anything?"

"Nothing yet."

Rithik turned to the next door on the right. He tried the handle, but it wouldn't budge. He took a step back and kicked it hard where the door latched. The latch broke and the door swung open. He entered the room, and there before him sat death. The withered corpse of his ancestor sat on a skeletal throne, his empty eyes staring skyward, ever searching … ever searching.

He woke to Waro's wet nose nudging his face.

Rithik was suddenly alert. "What is it?"

"Nothing," Waro said. "You were caught in a dream. You were trying to say something I couldn't understand."

Rithik couldn't remember what he would have been trying to say. He stretched and sat up.

Waro leaned his head into Rithik's shoulder. Despite his vocabulary, Waro's behavior still reflected some of the natural inclinations of his ancestors. Rithik put a hand to the dog's head and scratched his surprisingly soft ears. Waro's lips pulled back into a smile, and he leaned into Rithik even more.

"It's just as well," Rithik said. "We should keep moving."

"Dhere's more food," Waro said. "One could live comfortably here for a long while."

"It's certainly set up that way," Rithik said. "So where is everyone? If they died, where are their bodies? If they left, where did they go?"

"Dhe front door was open," Waro said. "Seems dhey went out."

"Maybe," Rithik said, getting to his feet. "But why?"

Waro sniffed the air as if for some answer, but made no comment.

Rithik packed some food and replenished their water. "We should keep searching," he said, and as soon as he was ready they set off, venturing into the maze of habitats that spiraled off the central hub.

11

Deep Medical

The corridors to Habitats A and B were sealed off, not far from the central hub. Heavy metal doors, like the quarantine door upstairs, blocked any further passage. In Habitat C they found nothing of interest. Several hours of exploration, corridor after corridor, door after door, revealed little else but an endless maze of domiciles, many showing signs of once having been lived in, but all abandoned.

Habitat E was different. The main corridor had many branching halls with endless domiciles like the ones they had seen already. But the main hall led to a secondary hub, and here they found passages marked *Power*, *Ecology*, and *Medical*.

Waro stopped and scratched behind an ear with his back foot. He stared up at the signs marking the corridors. "Which one?" he said.

Rithik pondered the options. *Power* was tempting. He imagined the depth of the ancients' magic, the power they must have commanded to build the cities above and all this below. *Ecology* was a word he did not know. But he knew the word *Medicine* and with the ghost flesh in him, he wondered if some medicine of the ancients might be his only hope.

"This way," Rithik said, and headed down the *Medical* corridor.

They passed through the smashed glass walls of an entry area. Scattered around the room inside, in various contorted positions of death, were around twenty skeletons. The most they had seen so far. Dust had gathered on the untouched bones and the scraps of dried withered flesh.

"Something sudden happened here," Rithik said. "Do you think some kind of disease killed them off?"

Waro sniffed one of the corpses, heedless of any imagined danger. He looked from corpse to corpse, many tangled together in groups. "Possibly," he said at last. "But some of dhese people just killed each other."

Rithik could see it now. Some of them had simple weapons clutched in their bony hands or lying nearby. Perhaps, in the midst of some crisis, they had busted in here and a fight broke out. In fear, in desperation, they had killed one another. But fear of what?

He looked beyond a further set of doors and found a wide corridor scattered with ancient corpses. Waro stopped by his side, sniffing at the musty air. And from there on they followed a trail of the dead.

Skeleton after skeleton marked the way, as if they had all died crawling toward the same thing, as if they had all perished on the same grim pilgrimage. Some appeared to have crushed ribs or broken backs. Others appeared to have simply dropped dead. Rithik and Waro stepped around them, leaving the twisted corpses undisturbed.

They passed by large, glass-walled rooms, perimeters lined with empty chairs, rooms and corridors beyond. They passed by office doors and vacant bathrooms. They passed through another pair of smashed glass doors, through another common area, and finally down long flights of winding stairs, where the corpses lay in piles on each landing.

Down and down they went, following the path of the doomed. There were ancient blood stains on the walls. There were scraps of clothing on the stairs. Darkness lay ahead of them, beyond the light of Rithik's torch, and darkness followed behind.

Waro bounded ahead onto a landing full of skeletons. He looked up at Rithik, as if about to ask a question, but said nothing.

Rithik reached the landing and rounded the corner. "Come on," he said. "They were obviously going somewhere." And he continued on.

"Dhat is what concerns me," Waro said as he followed Rithik down the next flight of stairs.

Deeper and deeper they went, until the final landing opened onto a large octagonal room. To the left was a bank of lift chute doors, all closed. To the right, three wide corridors branched off. The first was marked *Mutagenics*, the second *Pathology*. Both were sealed off with large quarantine doors. The third corridor was marked *Deep Medical*, and that is where the trail of bodies led.

Beyond the main corridor, Deep Medical appeared to be a maze of hallways, offices, and laboratories. The main path the residents of Evacuation Center Five had taken was still clear. Rithik followed, Waro at his side, with an increasing sense of dread. Here was death, plain to see, the great enigma, and maybe there was no answer. The ghost flesh itched and crawled beneath his skin. Maybe this path went on forever.

At last they came to a large lab of some sort. The outer steel doors were jammed open. The inner doors, made of glass, were smashed inward, shards of glass spread across the dusty floor. A few ancient skeletons, like the others, lay quiescent among the glass. Banks of equipment, cabinets, and large screens lined the perimeter. On the far side of the room, a large open doorway stood out, framed in thick metal. A line of flickering light ran around the inside of the door frame, but beyond was only darkness. It looked like that's where the people had gone.

Rithik advanced into the room cautiously, suddenly aware of the sword at his side, the pistol in his pocket, and the two remaining grenades that hung ready at his belt.

Waro hung back by the door, a few steps behind him.

Rithik scanned the long countertops. He touched several screens, tried the switches on some of the equipment, but everything here seemed dead, no power. He opened drawers and pulled out strange glass vessels, tubes, and boxes of gloves. He ransacked cabinets, pulling out ancient coveralls and masks, throwing them on the floor. He looked at some papers he found, shuffling through them, trying to make sense of the grids and marks and notes, and then frustrated, he threw them on the floor where they scattered amidst the bones.

"What are you looking for?" Waro said.

"Answers!" Rithik said. "I want answers!"

But there were none to be had. Not above, and not here. Rithik took a breath and calmed himself. A hunter always stayed calm, so he could see things clearly. How else would you find anything?

The flickering luminous doorway loomed in the darkness at the far side of the room. Rithik felt a chill breeze.

Waro growled.

In one quick motion, Rithik drew his sword. He took a step toward the doorway and half turned to Waro to reassure him. "Remember what you said. Ghosts can't harm you."

Waro took another step. "It's not ghosts dhat concern me."

Rithik advanced again slowly toward the luminous doorway. He could see a tunnel a few feet beyond cut out of the bare rock.

As he passed through the doorway, a string of make-shift lights came on, illuminating the twenty-foot length of the tunnel. Beyond that, again was darkness.

Rithik listened. He attuned all his senses to the task of perceiving something, anything, beyond, but aside from a slight chill in the air, he detected nothing.

Waro was at Rithik's heels, his ears tucked back, fur bristling, legs crouched, ready for anything.

Again, Rithik advanced, wary, and yet determined to go on.

At the end of the tunnel, the passage opened up into a natural cavern. Illuminated by his torch and the last of the tunnel lights, all Rithik could see was a bit of uneven ground, dotted with stalagmites. But somehow, the subtle echoes of his footsteps gave him an almost subconscious sense of a huge space within.

As he stepped into the cavern, two lights above him flickered on, and then two by two, more lights came on, arcing across the expanse on two cables fixed to a high rocky ceiling dotted with stalactites.

The lights appeared dim in contrast to the vast chamber they illuminated. The ground sloped downward in front of Rithik's feet, and below, across the floor of the huge cavern, was a pageant of death unlike anything Rithik had ever seen.

Thousands upon thousands of skeletons covered the ground, as if frozen in an endless desperate crawl toward the far side of the chamber. And there, where the long oval of the cavern narrowed and closed, tens of thousands were piled high on top of each other. The mass of skulls and bones sloped up from the cavern floor, culminating in a giant mound filling the entire end of the chamber. Rithik could make out a few individual skeletons frozen, as if in the midst of crawling on the mound of corpses, ever toward some unseen destination beyond the rocks. They had crawled over each other, across the backs of the dead and dying. They had clawed their way forward, ever forward, in a desperate pilgrimage to nowhere.

Rithik stared in awe and horror, and could utter but a single word, the whispered name of death's goddess.

"Yananna!"

12

Beyond the Cave of Bones

Under the dim lights flickering high overhead, Rithik and Waro wandered down into the cavern. By the time they were half way across the chamber it was impossible not to step on scattered bones. They had to pick their way carefully among the skulls of the ancients.

"Dhere is no other way out," Waro said when they had almost reached the edge of the massive bone pile.

Rithik looked back toward the tunnel that led to Evacuation Site Five. He scanned along the walls of the huge cavern and took in the whole morbid scene, from the bone littered floor to the sloping mountain of corpses that filled the far end of the chamber.

"They had to be going somewhere," Rithik said, staring at the mountain of death ahead of them. "There has to be a door or a passage or something beneath all those bodies."

He moved forward toward the sloping bone pile. Perhaps this was Yananna's cave, after all. He stopped at the edge of the corpse pile. From here they would have to climb over them, or …

"You're not dhinking what I am, are you?" Waro said.

"Maybe." Yes … they would have to dig through them.

Waro shook his head, a gesture more of disbelief than denial. "Digging is one dhing, and I admit to gnawing on a bone now and dhen, but dhis is something else."

"I know," Rithik said, "But there has to be a passage under there. It's a bottleneck. These are just the ones who didn't make it through."

"What makes you dhink dhe ones who made it fared better?"

"Something sent them down here. Maybe there's a way out." Rithik sheathed his sword and took a few steps forward, wading into the mass of bones. He started clearing a path through the bones with his feet. He picked up a skull and tossed it aside.

"Maybe dhere's a different way out," Waro said. "Did you dhink of dhat?"

Rithik turned and looked at Waro. He could feel the ghost flesh in his shoulder now, scrawling under the skin like a swarm of microscopic ants.

Waro sat and returned Rithik's gaze.

"Remember when we were in the desert," Rithik said, "and I asked you why you had followed me?"

Waro said nothing.

"You said it was a feeling you had."

Waro looked at him steadfast.

"Well ... do you still have that feeling?"

Waro huffed, shook himself all over, and started digging. And once he started, he left all scruples behind. With mouth and paw he dug with a kind of unbound scrappy enthusiasm.

Rithik threw aside bones and skulls and whole desiccated corpses. They dug through layer after layer, deeper and deeper into the mound. Time after time, stray bones, unsettled by the excavation, clattered down the pile and threatened to bury them.

After a long while, Rithik was covered in sweat and Waro was panting hard as they dug their way through the seemingly endless bones. They had made some progress, but were still far from the wall. They wouldn't make it in one shift, or even two, and so they sat down on the ground beyond the pile to eat something and quench their thirst.

For a while they sat, staring at the pile of bones. At some point in the last hour Rithik had become numbed to the morbidity of the task. He knew in his mind the bones had been people once, but they were just an obstacle now, a barrier keeping him from finding whatever lay beyond that wall. At this rate it could take a day, maybe more to dig through it all. Of course, he didn't know how much time he had before the ghost flesh took him. He didn't have time to waste.

Rithik stood up and gathered his things. "Waro, let's back up. I have an idea."

Waro trotted wearily back toward the tunnel without comment.

Rithik stopped some eighty feet from the bone pile and pulled a grenade from his belt. He looked at Waro.

"Dhat could cause a cave-in," Waro said, "Could bury dhis whole place."

Rithik had considered it. He figured a cave this big, that had been here for so long, should be stable. But the truth was, anything could happen. He didn't say anything, but he didn't pull the pin either. He waited to see if Waro would make any further objection.

Waro said nothing more. He sat and watched Rithik, waiting to see what he would do.

Rithik took a step toward the bone pile. Something was back there. Maybe it was the goddess Yananna. Maybe it was something else. Whatever it was, he was going to find it, or die trying.

He took a deep breath, pulled the pin, and threw.

The grenade clattered among the bones, high on the pile, and tumbled out of sight into some gap between them.

"Get down!" Rithik shouted.

Waro dropped to the ground and curled in a ball, his back to the bone pile. Rithik dropped to the ground hard and turned his head away.

The grenade went off with a deafening explosion, the concussive wave bouncing off every wall in the cavern. Bones and fragments of bones rained down on the ground around them. He listened for the sounds of falling rock but all he could hear was the ringing in his ears as he waited for the dust and debris to settle.

He turned his head to see what damage the grenade had done.

Waro howled with delight.

They had blown off the whole top of the mound! Many loose bones had fallen into the path they had already dug out, but it could be easily cleared and they would reach the back wall in no time.

Rithik sprang to his feet, ran ahead and started digging. Waro wasn't far behind.

They cleared away the collapsing heaps of bones, and dug with renewed vigor through the remaining pile. Old bones crunched beneath feet, hands, and paws. They dug faster and faster as they neared the wall, eager to discover what ancient secret remained there.

When they had finally cleared a path through the remains, at last they found what all these people had died to reach. It was a hole in the ground, not more than three feet across.

Rithik almost despaired to see that it too was filled with bones, but in the frenzy of his digging he just kept going, pulling out bone after bone until he broke through to a narrow, dark tunnel beyond.

So this was it. This was where they had all been going. Had they been mad? Had they been sick? What kind of insanity would drive people to kill each other, to trample one another to death, just to get to a hole in the ground? And how many could have passed through before they started piling up?

Rithik sat on the edge. He dropped his pack into the hole and climbed in after it. Once again, darkness reigned beyond the reach of his torch light. The tunnel was narrow enough that he had to crawl forward, pushing his pack ahead of him. He glanced back to see Waro jump into the hole behind him. The dog's eyes gleamed with torch light in the darkness.

Across the bare rock, on his hands and knees, Rithik crawled, occasionally banging his head on the ceiling. In a few tight spots he had to get down on his belly and inch forward like a worm. At those times, with nothing but a narrow tunnel of darkness ahead of him, Rithik felt like the pressure of the world, and the weight of his own existence, might crush him at any moment. It was a strange mixture of anxiety and inevitability, and all he could do was crawl on.

The tunnel branched multiple times with tiny passages snaking off into the eternal dark. Rithik always chose what looked like the largest passage, thinking, hoping, that the absence of corpses meant somebody must have made it through here in ancient times. At this point, there was nothing but hope to go on, but all things considered, what he really hoped for, he did not know.

13

Moth Maram

Rithik crawled forward for a long time. Waro followed, wiggling his way through the tunnel, never lagging or questioning what seemed like madness, to crawl ever deeper into the darkness, to venture ever onward into this underworld.

At last the tunnel widened, and eventually Rithik was able to stand again. His knees protested with pain as he stretched his legs. His hands were raw, his head battered, possibly bleeding, and every inch of his body ached. He leaned against the wall of the tunnel, ready to collapse.

"Keep moving," Waro said. "We'll rest when we see where dhis passage leads."

Where could it be going but to the end? Rithik wished, somehow, there *was* a way out, a way out other than *the* way out. But it seemed there was only the way through, through all the pain, the dread, the longing, and the heartbreak that was this life. There was only the way onward. And he was ashamed that this dog, who had followed him into the unknown, who would likely share his fate, would have to encourage him now. How could he still feel sorry for himself? So he pulled himself together. Expelling from his mind all thoughts of the future, he shouldered his pack and moved on.

In this perpetual darkness, there was no way to tell day from night, nor a minute from an hour. In his exhaustion his mind raced from one extreme to another as he watched the ground ahead of his footfalls.

"Look," Waro said. "Dhere's a light ahead."

Rithik looked up, but could see nothing except the torch light and the darkness beyond.

"Shut off your torch," Waro said.

Rithik turned the torch off and plunged them into a darkness from which it seemed no light could ever emerge. But after a few moments, he thought he saw something, a kind of dim green glow in the passage ahead. Was it his imagination?

"What is that?" Rithik whispered.

"I don't know," Waro said. "I hear something now too."

Rithik strained his ears but couldn't be sure if he heard anything. He took a few steps forward, feeling his way through the dark tunnel, lest he alert anyone ahead with his torch.

"Be careful," Waro said, following at his heels.

They advanced slowly. Soon Rithik could see the outlines of the tunnel ahead. He had to crawl again the last ten feet before he saw where the light was coming from.

They emerged into a huge natural cavern, larger than anything they had seen. It was immense. And all around, here and there, patches of stone were lit with green glowing lichens. The high vaults were riddled with shadowy contours, hanging ridgelines, and long stalactites. Below, at the bottom of a steep slope, was a stream, and the faint noise of the water flowing over the rocks echoed through the chamber.

For the moment, there was light enough to see by, and they zig-zagged their way down toward the stream, winding their way around house-size boulders covered with glowing lichens and giant stalagmites.

The clear water coursed through a shallow bed of smooth stone. Rithik flicked the switch on his chatter box and waved his hand across the water.

Nothing.

The water was free of ghosts. Perhaps down here there were no ghosts any longer. Perhaps this place was empty of memory and meaning. Perhaps it was free of the cataclysms of the ancient past.

He switched off the box and refilled his water bottle. He saw a fish swim out from underneath some rocks on the far shore. And not far from his feet, what looked like an overgrown click beetle navigated a forest of tall mushrooms.

Waro lapped up water at the stream's edge. He looked up, water still pouring from his slack jaw. He barked twice.

"Shh," Rithik said. "What is it?"

Waro craned his head back, sniffed at the air, and gazed across the broad ceiling. "I dhought I smelled something."

Rithik followed the dog's gaze, searching the patchwork of deep shadows and glowing lichens that covered the high vaults. He looked for any unusual shape, any sign of movement, but in such faint light, in the irregular undulating texture of the ceiling, one could see almost anything ... or nothing at all. He reached for his torch but wondered if it would do more harm than good, lighting up the immediate area, but blinding him to anything beyond it.

Then something passed before his eyes, some interruption in the pattern of light and shadow, somewhere between them and the ceiling.

Waro barked.

"Shhh!"

"I saw something."

"I saw it too." Rithik reached for his sword. He drew the ceramite blade slowly from its scabbard and held it ready. His left hand reached for the torch.

Again, something passed overhead, this time so close he heard a whisper in the air, and felt a breeze as it went by. What was it? Could Samsa, the great eagle, be here in this cavern? Was he even now delivering the dead to the temple of Yananna?

He crouched in waiting, sword ready, left hand poised to activate the torch.

A moment of stillness, then again something flew overhead.

Rithik turned on the torch.

Waro barked.

Rithik caught a glimpse of huge ghostly wings in the air, striated with black and pale green, with a large and hairy body beneath them. It disappeared in the darkness beyond the torch light almost as quickly as Rithik caught sight of it.

Waro barked and barked in the direction it had gone.

"Silence!" Rithik said.

Waro lowered his voice to a growl. His fur twitched and he bared his fangs and front teeth.

Rithik strained his eyes, searching the edge of the darkness.

Suddenly his vision filled with the flapping of huge wings, hairy dangling legs, large black eyes, and the furry bulbous bodies of giant moths. They were big as men, and dove in on erratic flight paths from every direction. Rithik raised his sword but was hit from behind. He stumbled forward, stepping into the water.

Waro barked furiously and turned in circles, his mouth snapping at the air as the moths fluttered overhead.

Another moth hit Rithik from the side, its huge legs wrapping around him for a moment. He tumbled over when it released him, dropping his sword and landing hard in the shallow water.

Rithik scrambled to his feet. Hordes of moths streamed in from the outer darkness, as if to smother them. He ducked as one flew at his head. The huge thing brushed his shoulder and flew out of the light once more.

He remembered the bolt pistol stowed in his vest pocket, and a moment later it was in his hand. He held the ancient weapon out, pointed it at the fluttering mass, and pulled the trigger. The thing jerked back in his hand and a loud report echoed through the cavern. But nothing happened. He must have missed.

He took aim with the pistol once more, waiting for a moth to fly into his sights.

Something struck the back of his hand, tearing through the flesh between his third and fourth finger. The pistol flew out of his grip. He steadied himself and found an arrow sticking halfway through his hand.

Blood started to seep from the arrow wound. Rithik looked up, confused and desperate to understand what was happening.

Out of the darkness, surrounded by a bursting halo of giant moths, a young woman walked toward him. In the light of his torch, her pale skin was as fine as gossamer. Her white hair was like strands of spider-silk, from which poked large pointed ears. Her almond-shaped eyes were unusually large and filled almost completely with black. Her nose was tiny, her lips thin, her mouth small. To Rithik's eyes, she was at once both shocking and beautiful.

She was naked to the waist, with a svelte torso and long limbs. She wore nothing but a leather loin cloth and soft soled shoes. Over her shoulder was slung a quiver of arrows. In her hands she held a bow, with another arrow already nocked to the string.

"Your light!" she said. "Turn off your light. It confuses them." She spoke the old tongue in a way Rithik had never heard before. Her accent, and even some of her words were strange.

Waro growled, folded his ears back, and took a step toward her.

She drew the bow string back, raised the tip of the arrow, and pointed it at Waro. "Stop right there, whatever you are, or this one goes through your eye."

"Easy, Waro," Rithik said. "It'll be all right."

"Now," she said. "Turn off your light."

Rithik raised his good hand slowly and switched the torch off.

It took a few moments for Rithik's eyes to adjust again to the relative darkness. Blood flowed from his hand, trickling in drops to the rocky ground. The wound throbbed.

In the dim green glow he could see the woman held her bow taut, and Waro still faced her in a standoff.

"We mean you no harm," Rithik said.

The woman didn't move.

"No harm," Rithik said. "Right, Waro?"

Waro took a single step back. His ears raised a bit and he tilted his head studying the woman.

The woman released the tension from her bow sting, but left the arrow still nocked.

"Who are you?" she said.

"I'm Rithik. I am a hunter from Tavala. Or I was at any rate. I suppose I'm nobody now."

"Tavala?" she said, testing the word in her mouth.

"Up there," Rithik said, motioning with his head, "above ground."

"Above ground." She merely repeated the words as if confused by their meaning.

"Outside," Rithik said, but could see she had no comprehension of the world outside.

"And you," she said to Waro, "What are you?"

Waro huffed. "I'm a dog, of course, and a wanderer in this world."

"You have disturbed the sanctuary. The sacred moths are guardians of the people. Nobody is allowed here except the Moth Maram, high priestess of the people.

"Sorry," Rithik said. "We meant no harm. We came by this place by accident. We know nothing of the moths or your people."

"I don't understand," she said, "How did you come to be here?"

"I was looking … for something," Rithik said.

"You do not speak the whole truth," she said, "But you are a truth speaker, a gentle soul." She returned the arrow she held to her quiver. "I've injured you. Let me tend to your wound."

14

CITY OF STONE

Rithik flinched as the woman took his wounded hand in hers. But it was only the sharpness of the pain. A person could not catch ghost flesh from an uninfected area. One could only catch it in the ruins or from the infected flesh of the dead. His wounded hand was not infected, and he was not a ghost yet.

She examined the wounds where the arrow entered and exited his hand. "I'm sorry," she said. "I was only protecting the moths."

"It's all right," Rithik said. "Apparently we are the trespassers here. I'm just glad your aim is good."

Waro groaned, lay down on the rocks, and watched the woman closely.

The woman unshouldered her quiver and opened a compartment on the bottom. From it she took some strips of soft leather, a wad of what looked like dried moss, a bone needle, a dowel wound with silk thread, and a tiny covered clay pot.

From her hip she drew a stone blade, and with it she quickly stripped the fletches from the arrow in Rithik's hand.

"I'm Laila," she said, "Moth Maram of the people." There was no pride in her voice, though the title seemed important.

Rithik's mind filled with questions. Was she a spirit or human-born? Who were these people? Where had they come from? How long had they lived here? But just as he was about to start asking, she pulled the arrow through his hand with one quick motion.

Rithik made a noise, but mindful of his pride as a hunter, he quickly silenced himself.

Laila examined his hand. Fresh blood flowed from the wounds, but it did not spurt.

"Can you move these fingers?" she said.

Rithik bent his third and fourth fingers a little, but the pain was great.

"You're lucky," Laila said. "Go wash it in the swift water."

Rithik did as he was told and returned to where Laila sat among patches of luminescent lichens.

She took his hand in hers once more.

"No stitches," she declared. "This type of wound is best left open to heal. We'll wrap it for now."

She wadded some of the dried moss together into a pad and wrapped it around the bottom half of his hand. Then she took a long strip of soft leather and bound it carefully. When she finished she sat and simply stared at Rithik and Waro in silence.

"Thank you … Laila," Rithik ventured.

The faintest trace of a smile passed across her closed lips, but it quickly vanished. She was thinking. She was debating what to do with them.

Finally, she spoke. "As children we all heard the stories of outsiders, but you do not seem wicked. You are strange looking for sure … both of you. But you're not like the grimlocks, and you do not seem like a threat to the people."

"We mean no harm" Rithik said.

"We are only travelers," Waro said, "passing dhrough."

"Your hand will need looking after," Laila said. "It is my responsibility. I can take you to the temple, where you can rest and heal. Will you come?"

Rithik nodded.

Laila turned to Waro. "And you, Waro?"

"Of course," Waro said. "Where else would we go?"

"You must promise to be quiet," Laila said. "Many of the people will be afraid if they hear an outsider has come. I must have time to explain what has happened."

"I promise," Rithik said.

"And you must not turn on your light. It is like the lights of Maitreyu, far too bright for the people."

"Agreed," Rithik said.

"Then follow me."

In the dim glow of the luminescent lichens, Laila led them upstream. Waro seemed to follow behind Rithik as much by smell as by sight. His head hung low, sniffing everything as he walked.

"This way," Laila said, skipping effortlessly across the stream on the backs of a few large rocks protruding from the water.

Rithik followed carefully, jumping from rock to rock.

Waro waded through the stream without deliberation, shaking himself off on the far shore.

They made their way across a field of flowstone to the other side of the cavern, and climbed a rocky slope to where the walls narrowed. Laila was as lithe as a yarcat as she danced up the rocks, periodically stopping to wait for Rithik and Waro to catch up. Occasionally, Rithik caught a glimpse of a giant moth fluttering through the air in the darkness overhead, or clinging to the mass of a low hanging stalactite.

As they reached the edge of the cavern, Laila led them into a room filled with slender natural columns. The dim light from the lichens grew ever dimmer, but Rithik could still see what looked like dark tunnels branching off from the edges of the room.

"Stay close," Laila said as she ducked into one of them.

Upon entering the tunnel, Rithik was immediately plunged into absolute darkness. He banged his head against the low ceiling, stumbled, tripped, hit his knee, and scrambled forward blindly.

He heard strange clicking sounds ahead, but could see nothing. Laila had completely disappeared in the darkness. He could feel Waro sniffing at his heels and he groped his way forward through the dark.

He wanted to turn his light on, just on low, but he had promised not to. A hunter keeps his promises, and so does not promise lightly.

Hoping it was Laila, he headed toward the clicking sound he heard up ahead.

The clicking sounds grew fainter and then louder. Then suddenly, he felt a hand on his shoulder. Startled, he stood upright, hit his head again, and cursed in the darkness.

"What are you doing?" It was Laila's voice.

"I can't see a damn thing in here."

"You can hear, can't you?"

"Yes but ..."

Laila made two short clicking sounds, and then laughed. "You mean, you cannot hear the walls of the tunnel ... or the shape of my face before you?"

He could sort of feel how close she was, and he could hear her voice, but that was all. He never imagined one could hear walls or faces. All at once, he realized Laila was experiencing something entirely different than he was. She sensed her surroundings, as if seeing, in the echoes of their voices and the clicking sounds she made in the darkness. He could not imagine what this would *look* like to her, but it was clear she was doing it.

"What about your friend?" Laila said.

"I can't hear dhe walls," Waro said, "but I can smell my way just fine."

Rithik felt ashamed of his own inability to navigate the darkness.

"Here," Laila said, "take my arm, and keep your head down."

Her arm, now Rithik's lifeline, was thin and muscled beneath the fingers of his wounded hand. He moved forward, feeling the ground with his feet, and veering this way and that according to the movement of Laila's arm. He tried to move as fast as he could. After a while he stumbled along with some proficiency, but he could tell he was slowing Laila down.

They made several lefts and rights, went up a ways and then down even farther. Rithik was now hopelessly lost if he hadn't been already. But he had no thoughts of going back. He would go ever forward, ever searching until the end. For what, if not Yananna herself, he did not know, but he would go on until he found it. Or until the ghost flesh took him.

"Stay against the wall on your left here," Laila said. "There's a drop-off just to the right."

Rithik felt along the wall with his left hand, and walked as close as he could to it. He felt a movement in the air, a warm, humid breeze coming up from below and to his right. He pictured a deep dark pit of immense depth, with faint traces of steam rising from below.

"Waro, are you there?" Rithik said.

"I'm fine," Waro said. "Keep to your left."

They kept moving. After a ways Laila moved to the right. Rithik resisted, the image of a drop-off still in his mind.

"It's all right," Laila said. "It's safe here. The dropoff is far behind us now."

Rithik exhaled, realized he had been holding his breath, and left the wall he had clung to. He noted that in the darkness his mind would play tricks on him. He could not avoid trying to form an image of his surroundings, but any image he held on to could quickly get him into trouble.

"I smell people," Waro said. "Many people ahead."

"We are almost to the dwellings," Laila said. "You must be silent until we reach the temple. I do not wish to draw attention."

Rithik said nothing. But when they rounded a turn in the passage, even he could tell they had come out into another huge cavern. The temperature rose. He could feel the air move, and there was something about the echoes of their feet and the distant sounds that played at his mind, creating half-formed images of an immense chamber spreading out before and below them.

Were those voices he heard in the distance? They were the clicks and shouts of Laila's people, living here in the darkness among the rocks. He heard the bubbling of running water too, far off toward what he imagined was the center of the cavern. He pictured a village surrounding a stream, a village of stone houses, and pale, waif-like people, clicking their way down lanes and alleys.

"Quickly," Laila whispered, "or the people will hear you."

Rithik picked up his pace, following beside Laila, trying to keep his feet under him. The ground was smoother here, as if they walked along a long established path. They were going down, perhaps somewhere along the edge of this huge cavern.

They made several switchbacks, turning left and then right, and then left again.

At last Laila paused, but she quickly pushed Rithik against a rock wall. "Silence," she whispered. Rithik felt Waro up against the wall next to him.

A man's voice in the darkness called out, "Who is that there?"

The man was not far off, perhaps on an intersecting path.

Laila answered, "Greetings, Profham. It is only I, Laila, returning from the sanctuary."

"Ah, moth hara, Moth Maram," the voice said, in a kind of benediction. Then he added, "Is there someone there with you?"

"No, Profham, it is only me."

Rithik stood flat against the wall and hoped their presence would not cause trouble. The silence seemed to draw out unbearably.

"Good waking and sleeping to you, then. I am past due at home. Oura will be waiting for me."

Laila remained still on the pathway. Rithik could hear the man moving off. When he was gone they continued on their way.

Finally, Laila stopped. "We're here," she said. "Come. You can rest inside the temple. Nobody can enter here without my permission."

Laila led them forward. They slid past what felt like three heavy leather curtains. Inside, the air was still and warm, and the darkness seemed closer around them. It was a kind of room or small chamber. Laila led him through the room, past another curtain and into what felt like a slightly larger room. The floor was smooth and almost flat.

"Here," Laila said, "You can sit here and lie down if you like."

Rithik felt a stone platform, covered in soft fur. He sat down and ran his hands along the edge. It was a kind of alcove that served as a couch or a bed. There were leather pillows at either end.

"And here, Waro, you may recline on these furs."

Rithik listened to Laila fuss over making Waro comfortable.

Waro made no protest. He settled in and thanked her.

"I have food and drink if you're wanting," Laila said.

"Thank you," Rithik said, "but maybe I'll just rest for now." He felt exhausted. As he leaned back into the soft furs and put his head upon the pillow, he realized he had not been so comfortable since leaving Tavala. Though his wounded hand still throbbed, he took a deep breath, and momentarily forgot all his troubles. Soon, he was fast asleep.

15

WHISPERS IN THE DARK

Rithik dreamt about his sister. It was early spring that year when Praya fell ill with the winter sickness. She had been in bed a week with a high fever and a bad cough.

The snows were thawing and the runoff usually carried with it some good finds. Rithik was planning an artifact hunting expedition at the upper edge of the river city. Three other young hunters were going, and he would take the lead. Praya sent for him the night before they were to set out.

She looked pale, even in the warm light of the candle lantern by her bedside. A charcoal brazier burned in the corner, and despite the heat, Praya shivered beneath the thick covers of her bed.

Rithik sat by her side.

Her cheeks looked hollow, her eyes wide.

They talked of events in Tavala. When the subject of his expedition came up, she begged him not to go.

Rithik would not be swayed though. Everything was ready, and he had a responsibility to the other hunters. He thought Praya was just being dramatic. She would surely get better soon.

Finally she broke down and wept. "I'm scared, Rithik." Her weeping turned into a coughing fit that lasted almost a minute.

Rithik took her hand and tried to reassure her. "I'll only be gone a few days," he said. "I'll look for something special for you in the ruins. You'll be better in no time, and I'll be back before you know it. You'll see."

That was the last time he saw her alive.

Rithik woke. He opened his eyes, but there was no change, not a single glimmer of light in the darkness. He remembered where he was, inside Laila's temple, but with no picture, no other sensation, the space seemed more like a thought than an actual place.

He heard something stir a few feet from where he was. That must be Waro. Still, they could be anywhere. They could be lost in endless cave tunnels. They could be in the spirit realm already. They could be in Yananna's cave.

There was someone else there. He started to sit up, felt and remembered the fur of the bedding, the soft pillow, the pain in his hand, and a picture of the room began to form once more.

"Oh, you're awake," Laila's said, across the room to his left.

"Did I sleep long?"

"A long time," Waro said, still next to the platform.

"You slept all through the sleeping," Laila said. "It is now waking again for the people. How is your hand?"

Rithik flexed his hand slightly. The pain was intense but bearable.

"Try not to move it," Laila said. "It needs time for the tissue to heal."

He could hear her crossing the room toward him.

"Here," she said, sitting beside him. "Drink this."

Laila's slender hands held a warm ceramic bowl. Careful not to spill it in the darkness, he took the bowl from her and drank. The contents tasted like an earthy sort of tea, bland but invigorating.

"Moss tea," Laila said. "Finish it while you wait. I am preparing fresh gharbat, grubs, and lichens for you to eat."

She rose again and crossed the room. Rithik heard her doing things, but could see nothing.

"It smells good," Waro said. "Your kindness speaks well of your people."

Rithik had his doubts about grubs and gharbat, but he was so hungry by the time Laila handed him a plate full of food that he ate it all without hesitation. He scooped soft grubs, some kind of meat, and papery sheets of lichen into his mouth with gusto, washing it all down with more moss tea.

When he had finished, Laila arranged the leather pillows so he could recline against the stone wall. Once he was settled she sat next to him, her bare arm touching his, and her soft hip pressed against him in the darkness.

Rithik's heart raced, despite his desire to remain objective. In Tavala this would be a very intimate situation. But he was not in Tavala anymore, and things were very different here.

"Tell me about the outside," Laila said.

"You've never been outside?"

"Nobody here has ever been outside. There are stories, of course, and long ago they say our people came from the outside. But they are only stories. Many people do not believe it exists."

Rithik tried to imagine these people living down here in the darkness for generations. Were they descended from the ancients? Could they have evolved from the people of Evacuation Center Five? It seemed possible. But who could say?

"Does it exist?" Laila said, pressing him for an answer.

"Yes," Rithik said, although under the present circumstances, he could almost doubt it himself. "Far above here the ground opens up to the sky, the sun and moon and stars. And in the light of day you can see for miles and miles."

"You use so many strange words. What is the sky?"

"It's like … there is no ceiling overhead, no vault of stone."

She gripped his arm. "What is there then?"

"Clouds … endless space."

"It sounds terrifying."

"Oh … no … it's quite beautiful."

"You said you were looking for something," Laila said. "What are you looking for?"

Rithik took a breath. How could he explain? He could barely explain it to himself. "This wound in my hand," he said, "is the least of my troubles. I have what we call ghost flesh, here in my other arm. It's a kind of infection I caught in the ruins of the outside world. It will spread until it kills me. There is no cure. But I'm looking … I'm looking for answers, I guess."

"Oh," she said. "How long …"

"I don't know. A week. Maybe a month, I don't know."

"You thought you would find answers here?"

"Where I come from, we believe an eagle carries the dead to the cave of Yananna, goddess of the underworld. She cleanses them of world corruption and prepares their souls for rebirth. I came here seeking Yananna's cave. I thought maybe …" But really, he didn't know what he thought. Nothing made sense any more.

"I have never heard of this goddess."

Rithik laughed. "It was a foolish idea anyway. Yananna's cave is in the spirit realm."

"Perhaps Maitreyu will know where it is," she said. Then she put a hand on his. "Perhaps Maitreyu will know a cure for your sickness."

Rithik sat up. "Who is this Maitreyu?"

There was a shout from somewhere beyond the room.

"Shh," Laila said. "Be silent. If I must go, stay here until I return."

She rose and Rithik listened as she crossed the room, and slid past the leather curtains that separated this room with the outer vestibule chamber.

Beyond the vestibule, he heard Laila speaking with somebody. He tried to make out what they were saying, but their voices were too faint and muffled by the curtains. They spoke for a few moments, and then nothing. In the distance Rithik heard only silence now. The ghost flesh itched in his shoulder and he scratched at it. Right in front of his face, he knew only darkness, the darkness that was already here, and the one that was coming.

16

Relics of a Bygone Age

While Rithik slept, Laila had shown Waro around the small cave where she lived. So now, as Rithik groped his way through the room trying to form a mental picture of the place, Waro provided a stream of ongoing commentary.

Rithik took a step into the darkness and stubbed his toe, half doubling over in pain.

"Watch out for dhat step dhere," Waro said.

Thinking better of his plan to walk across the room, Rithik returned to the wall and groped along it. His foot ran into something … not rock … not …

"Dhat's me, you idiot."

He carefully stepped around Waro and continued, feeling his way along the wall. On his next step, the wall vanished, and his hand thrust into a darkness that seemed poised to envelop him. He almost fell.

"Careful, dhere's a passage dhere."

"Thanks for mentioning it," Rithik said.

"Dhat leads to the temple of moths."

Rithik skipped the gap and again continued along the wall, until his hand knocked over a stack of ceramic bowls.

"And dhat's the kitchen," Waro said.

"Look, maybe you can just show me around. Like, for example, is there a place I could take a leak around here?"

It was a relief to hear that there was. Waro led him through the curtains into the vestibule, and then down a small narrow passage that developed a distinctive smell the further they went. Waro stopped. "Don't take another step! Dhere's a hole dhere, straight ahead. You can't miss."

With that important business taken care of, Rithik made his way back to the main room. All his things, his gear and his weapons, were where he left them by the bed, but he still could not picture the place. He had a feeling the image he held was distinctly different from the reality that existed.

Rithik sat down by his gear. He propped a leather pillow behind his back and sighed. Waro curled up on the ground next to him. In the absolute darkness, Rithik felt like he was looking at the contents of his own mind. Whatever thoughts arose, whatever memories he had, whatever dreams he once held onto, there they were, like ghosts in the darkness. "Waro," he said, "What are we doing here?"

Waro huffed and creaked out a yawn. "Do you mean in the immediate sense, or the philosophical sense?"

"In any sense whatsoever."

"Rithik, long ago, in the wastelands, I gave up trying to make sense of it all. I am a wanderer. I made my peace with life and death. And so, wherever I go, I am just wandering here and dhere. But you, I feel, you are still looking for something."

Rithik's heart clenched. Tears threatened to well up in his eyes. He clutched himself and shook with unspeakable longing. "I just ... I just want ..." But he couldn't say what it was. There was no name for what he longed for. It was too vast. It was beyond the words of any tongue.

"When you're looking for something," Waro said, "you must keep searching until your search is over."

Rithik wiped the tears from his eyes and took a deep breath. He supposed there really was nothing to do but go on, as Waro said. To search ever deeper until he could search no more, or until he found what he was looking for. There was nothing to do but go on to the end, to whatever end fortune gave him, to whatever end judgment held for him, to whatever end.

After a few moments, Rithik rummaged around in his gear. He donned his belt and vest, and made sure his pack was secure. "I need to see this place," he said. "I need to really see it. I need to look around."

"What do you mean?"

Rithik found his torch and readied to turn it on. "We're in a cave, right? I mean this area is closed off from the cavern beyond. There are at least four curtains and a ninety degree turn between here and the entrance."

"Remember you promised not to use your light."

"Only because of the danger someone would see it." Rithik stood up. "Nobody will see it here. I'll put it on low and shield it behind my vest."

Waro got to his feet. He made no further comment.

Rithik turned the torch on low, and suddenly there was light.

After the absolute darkness, even on low, the torch seemed incredibly bright. Rithik hid it behind the lapel of his vest. It glowed through the fabric, illuminating the surroundings in a soft beige light.

They stood in a space that was smaller than Rithik had imagined. It looked like a natural cave, but one that had been cleaned out and customized for living. The rough natural ceiling was largely untouched, but the floors had been leveled off in many places. Here and there, alcoves had been chiseled out of the walls for the bed and for storage. The kitchen had flat counter surfaces and a basin filled with warm water that seemed to flow continuously from a small hole drilled into the wall. The excess water flowed away along a channel at the back of the counter, down along the side, and disappeared into a natural gap in the floor.

The curtain covering the door into the vestibule was indeed made of some kind of soft, thin leather. He didn't want to risk going that way with the lantern, but there was the other passage that Waro had said led to the temple. He took a step into the passage, which spiraled down and around to the left.

"Are you sure we should enter here?" Waro said. "It seems to have religious significance."

"Just to look," Rithik said. "We should learn as much as we can about these people."

"All right, dhen," Waro said. "Just a look."

Rithik continued down the passage. The floor had been worn down over many years into what amounted to natural steps. The passage descended, then curved back to the right and opened up into a cavern at least three times as large as the bedroom.

To the right, the cavern extended into a large open space, with a passage at the far end. To the left, wide natural steps rose into a round, high-vaulted chamber.

Rithik went left, ascending the natural stairs to the circular, roughly domed chamber above. Before him, in a large alcove, was a giant moth. Rithik crouched, ready to defend himself, although he realized he left his weapons in the other room. The moth, in any case, didn't move, and after a few moments, Rithik figured it must be dead.

"An object of veneration," Waro ventured.

Rithik approached the huge moth, examined its striped wings, furry legs, and large antennae. The wings were frayed around the edges, hinting that this specimen had been here a long time.

Waro sniffed at the base of the alcove. "Look, here's dhe same glowing lichen we saw in dhe moth cave."

Sure enough, and when Rithik switched off his torch, the cool glow of the lichen illuminated the alcove. In the faint light the moth looked alive again, and Rithik could see why the people here would venerate such a creature. Here, indeed, was the goddess of all moths.

"Perhaps this is a realm of spirits, after all," Rithik said.

"Having never been to dhe spirit realm," Waro said. "How will you know when you have arrived?"

For a moment Rithik regarded the giant moth, and pondered Waro's strange question. He had no answer, and after a moment he turned to examine the rest of the chamber.

With his light off now, he noticed something else he hadn't seen when they entered the room. There was more lichen glow coming from a narrow passage on the left side wall.

"This way," Rithik said, stepping into the passage. Again the passage wound down steeply and to the left. After a few feet, glowing lichens grew here and there on the walls, and Rithik had no need to turn on his light. At the bottom they emerged into a small room below the moth chamber.

Rithik's breath stopped, and stuck deep in his lungs.

Treasure!

Hanging from the walls, heaped in corners, were a multitude of ancient artifacts, some of which Rithik had never seen before, even in the markets at Pithtek. Power cells and lanterns, com-boxes and medical supplies, power tools, ceramite armor, power goggles, and drug bottles. And more screens than Rithik had ever seen in one place. They littered the room like two dimensional jewels, reflecting the dim light of the glowing lichens that clung to the ceiling and walls. And there, at the head of the room, hanging on the wall, was a Mark IV laser cannon in pristine condition, complete with a combat power pack. Treasure of treasures!

"Well, look at that," Rithik said, finally managing to exhale.

An artifact like that was the dream of hunters everywhere. Its power was beyond measure. Its value too, could probably feed the population of Tavala for a generation or more if one could manage to sell it without getting killed first. Most of these things had disappeared or been destroyed, one way or another, in olden times, in the dark years that followed the fall of the ancients. Except for this one, which had probably been here ever since.

"They must have brought these things with them, when they came here from above," Rithik said. He reached out toward the Mark IV laser. "I wonder if it still works."

Laila's voice stopped him. "Rithik?"

"Uh oh," Waro said.

Rithik turned to make for the exit, but there was only one way in or out, and they could already see Laila's feet as she stepped down into the room.

"You should not be down here," she said when she found them.

"I'm sorry," Rithik said.

"It's my fault," Waro said. "I dhought I smelled something."

"Maybe the others are right about outsiders," Laila said. But when she looked at Rithik in the dim lichen-glow, she failed to conjure an expression of genuine anger.

"What is this place?" Rithik said.

"These are the things we left behind," Laila said. "These are the relics of ancient times. As the Moth Maram, I keep them and the knowledge of them. There is too much light in them for the people. I alone must bear the burden."

"Where I come from, some of these relics are great treasures."

"There is no treasure here except the life of the people. The light of Maitreyu is too much for the people. Even the light of Moth Reyla is too bright, while the darkness of the lower caves is too grim. We have found contentment here. And here we shall remain."

It sounded like a saying, something she had been taught as a child, some teaching of the people. Again, Rithik recognized the name of Maitreyu, and now Moth

Reyla. Perhaps they were gods. The dream dwellers talked of many gods, not just Yananna. Although he had never heard of one called Maitreyu.

"I'm not sorry you've come," Laila said. She looked at Waro and then at Rithik. "So little changes here … and sometimes I dream of change. I know it's wrong, but sometimes I dream of a light brighter than anything anyone has ever seen. Have you ever seen such a light?"

"The sun."

"You must tell me all about it. Come though, let us talk in my room." She took Rithik's hand, even though there was still light to see by, and led him up the passage and out into the temple. But there in the hall beyond the temple they met a throng of at least thirty or forty people.

They were dressed as Laila was, both men and women, with belts and leather loin cloths. Their hair was long, and elaborately braided. Their eyes were large, although many squinted or held them shut against the dim glow of the lichens.

For a moment, they stood in awe and terror. Some gazed through narrowed eyes. Some clicked and saw with open ears.

Then someone shouted, "Outsider!" and the whole throng seemed about to charge.

17

The People

"He's got the Moth Maram!"

"I knew I heard someone!"

"What is that there?" someone yelled, as Waro came into view.

"A monster!"

The crowd seethed forward in a confused mob. Their faces filled with horror, loathing, anger, and perhaps worst of all, fear. They did not look like violent people, but in this state and in these numbers, they looked capable of anything.

Waro bared his teeth and growled, making matters worse.

Laila held up her hands and shouted, "It's all right. It's all right. These are friends!" But in the chaos they could not hear her, or simply didn't hear her over the cacophony of their own fear and anger.

There was nowhere to run to without running into the masses.

The men in front lurched forward as if preparing to attack Rithik.

"Your light," Laila said. "Turn on your light!"

Rithik grabbed his torch and turned it on full. Light blasted through the chamber, stark and glaring, like a sheet of lightning that did not end.

The people shrieked. Even those with closed eyes covered their eyes with their arms and hands, shielding themselves from the light that penetrated their eyelids. They staggered backward, dumbfounded with awe and terror.

Even Rithik's eyes recoiled at the intensity of the light, but Laila walked forward into it and held out her arms for all to see or hear. "My people," she said. "Have no fear. Your Moth Maram is safe and free from harm. These visitors have no ill will. Now depart from the temple and disperse."

She signaled to Rithik, and he turned the torch off.

They were once again plunged into the relative darkness, but the mass of people were subdued. Some backed out the door with heads bowed. Others still cowered in the darkness. Three of the braver ones, or perhaps the leaders, seemed to study Laila, who stood now between them and Rithik.

"Go, Kethan," Laila said. "Out beyond the temple threshold, and I will tell you all that has transpired."

The three men bowed reluctantly and backed up, following the others beyond the outer passage.

Laila turned to Rithik and Waro. "I'm sorry," she said. "I had hoped to avoid this, but I was foolish to think I could hide you from the people. Go back to my room and wait there for me. And this time, don't go anywhere."

Rithik nodded, and watched Laila depart into the darkness of the passage beyond the hall. Then he followed Waro back up into Laila's room. And there they waited.

Rithik heard Waro flop down on the ground, and huff a sigh of relief. A moment later he squeaked out a yawn while Rithik paced the room. He walked in the darkness from one unseen wall to other. The ghost flesh crawled at his skin, and he wondered, would they find sanctuary here, or would he once again be set out beyond the pale? What was worse, to find death in the wilderness, beneath the sun and moon and stars, or to wander in this labyrinth of tunnels, in this darkness, forever? It was too late now. Too late.

For a long time they waited. Rithik suspected Waro had gone to sleep, and wondered how he could sleep after that scene in the temple, when the fate of their journey seemed to hang on what would happen next.

At last Laila returned, her voice at once businesslike and reassuring. "I have told the elders everything. They wish to interview you both immediately. Leave your weapons. They will be safe here. The people are afraid but will not harm you. I promise."

Waro got to his feet in the darkness.

Rithik left his belt, his sword and knife, the pistol, and his last grenade. But he kept his torch in its mesh pocket, just in case.

"Take my arm," Laila said. "I will guide you."

Outside the temple caves, Rithik felt the presence of people once more. They stayed back, but he heard their clicks and whispers. A crowd of them clambered over the nearby rocks and followed, as Laila led him and Waro down, deeper into the cavern of the dwellings.

The air became warmer, almost steamy as they descended along a well-worn path. By the time Laila guided them into a passage veiled with more leathery curtains, Rithik had broken a sweat.

The chamber inside was as dark as the cavern outside. It seemed larger than Laila's room, but smaller than the temple hall. In the darkness, Rithik could only guess what it looked like.

"Sit here," Laila said, and guided him to a hard leather cushion on the rocks.

Rithik sat down cross-legged on the cushion and tried to make himself comfortable.

"In front of you sit the four elders," Laila said, "They are the leaders and the wisdom of the people."

Someone made several loud clicks and in the silence that followed an old man spoke.

"One of you is human, but the other is a form unknown to us. What manner of creature are you?"

"I'm a dog," Waro said, "not dhat dhere's much in dhe word to understand. Call me Waro. I am just a wanderer. I seek no trouble, nor anything else."

"Then you must be the one called Rithik."

Rithik could feel the old man direct his full attention on him, even in the total darkness.

"I am," Rithik said. "We thank you for your hospitality. Laila—the Moth Maram—has been kind to us. How shall we address you?"

There was no response.

"The elders have given up their names," Laila said. "They are only the elders.

"You are outsiders," another old voice said harshly. "From where have you come?"

"From a village called Tavala, outside, above ground."

"Above ground you say?"

"How long has it been," Rithik said, "since you have seen an outsider here?"

The elders grumbled and whispered among themselves. Finally the first one spoke again.

"There has never been an outsider here among the dwellings. From the time our ancestors came to this place until now, you are the first."

"The outsiders took in too much light," another old voice said.

"They destroyed the world above, the world outside," another said. "There is nothing left."

Rithik had no desire to debate what was left of the outside world. After all, what difference did it make to him now? And yet … "Nevertheless," he said, "that's where we came from."

"Will more outsiders come now?" the first old man said.

"We are alone," Rithik said.

"*Why* did you come, then?"

Again, Rithik struggled to find an answer. "I seek the cave of Yananna, goddess of death and rebirth." It sounded crazy, even to him, when he said it out loud. But it was the truth. Why else had he come this far? He did not want to die, and if anyone could spare him it was death herself.

The elders again whispered among themselves, their voices barely audible.

"You have put us between two rocks," the old man said. "But such is the way of the people. The old stories have made us wary of outsiders. However, the Moth Maram has spoken for you and we shall abide by her wish. Let Maitreyu guide us. He will know the place you seek, and if he commands, we will make a place for you in the dwellings where you may live in peace."

"What does it mean?" Rithik said. "Who is this Maitreyu?"

"None can compare to the Lord of Lights," one of the other elders said wistfully, as if conjuring an ancient memory.

"You will see for yourself," the old man said. "The Moth Maram will take you at soonest waking. Our hunters will see you safely through the lower caverns."

Hunters, Rithik thought, one more expedition of hunters. He didn't know whether to laugh or cry. One way or another, he felt certain it would be his last.

18

THE LOWER CAVES

Laila woke Rithik at dawn. Well, it felt like dawn in any case. It seemed he had hardly slept, and the darkness he woke to was the same as his dreams.

"Come with me," Laila said.

Rithik followed her into the moth temple, where they stood in the light of the alcove beneath the great moth.

"Give me your hand," she said.

Rithik held out his wounded right hand.

Laila removed the wrapping and examined the wound. From a pouch at her side she produced an ancient medi-strip. Rithik had seen one when he was younger, but they were too valuable for the people of Tavala to keep or use. They could heal deep wounds in a matter of minutes.

Laila tore open the packaging on the medi-strip. She removed the backing and took Rithik's hand. She stuck one half of it over the wound on the back of his hand, and wrapped it around so the other half covered the wound on his palm. A shimmering light passed across the back of the medi-strip, and Laila held his hand in hers.

The pain was gone immediately, followed by a soft, tingling sensation.

"There," she said. "Now whatever happens, my heart will rest easy. I wish I could do more."

"Your kindness has already exceeded all expectations," Rithik said.

Laila smiled. "Come, fetch your gear and wake Waro from his sleep. The hunters await us."

Outside the temple complex, Laila greeted several people who had gathered. To Rithik, she said, "These hunters will escort us through the lower caves. Their names are Kethan, Hanlo, and Eck."

"Moth Maram says you are a hunter yourself," one of them said.

Rithik recognized the voice from the leaders of the mob in the temple. "I was a hunter of Tavala when I lived there."

"Good," the man said. "There are gharbats in the lower caves. Maybe you'll show us your technique."

Suddenly Rithik felt like a novice again, learning to scavenge in the edges of the ruins, ignorant from one danger to the next. He wasn't going to say he wasn't a hunter any more, and in any case he had never been that kind of hunter, except out of necessity. But instead he said, "Sure thing."

"Gharbats are nothing," Waro said. "You should try hunting ubok."

Rithik stifled his laugh. If the silence of the others was any indication, they weren't sure what to make of Waro or his comment. They had clearly never seen a lumbering, fat, grass-grazing ubok or they would have been less impressed.

"Right," one of them said tentatively. "Well, let's go."

They descended into the cavern of the dwellings, and departed by some side passage the best Rithik could tell. Although his ability to walk blindly through the caves was improving, from the outset, he was surely slowing them down as he fumbled along with Laila guiding him. Still, she declined the few times he had offered to light their way.

They passed through seemingly endless tunnels, large caverns and small, with echoing vaults, and even some glowing lichens, where the hunters shielded their eyes and Laila scanned the high stalactites for any sign of moths. They passed through a large chamber filled with the endless roar of a waterfall, which Laila said marked the upper end of the lower caves. For half a day or more they traveled before breaking for water and a light meal. The hunters continued to talk about gharbats, but they hadn't spotted any.

They had climbed down into a large, long cavern that stretched out ahead of them. Was it Rithik's imagination, or was he starting to form some image of their surroundings from the echo of their footsteps and the clicks of the hunters, from Laila's voice and Waro's panting? The vaults of this chamber were at least a hundred feet or more overhead.

The hunters stopped. "Gharbats," one of them said. Rithik could practically hear them smiling.

"This isn't a hunting expedition," Laila said.

"Moth Maram, this may be our best chance, and the people could use the meat and hide."

Laila said nothing.

Hunters were the same everywhere, Rithik thought. They couldn't help themselves.

"Rithik, do you want to call one in?" One of the hunters baited him.

Despite himself he was starting to like these guys. They reminded him of his old hunting party from Tavala, always goading each other into ever more foolhardy acts. He had no idea how to call in a gharbat, but on a whim he let out a long low howl that echoed through the vast chamber.

The hunters laughed.

"Wait! There, one dropped!"

"It's coming this way."

"Hanlo, track it."

Hanlo let out a series of loud sharp clicks. Rithik heard the others quickly nock arrows. The bows creaked taught. There was a rustling sound, a hot wind, and arrows flew.

A monstrous creature shrieked in darkness, and thudded to the ground just beyond them.

The hunters cheered and quickly hushed themselves to find their quarry.

"It's a big one! Thanks to Rithik we will feast tonight."

The hunters celebrated, but Laila did not move. She stood perfectly still. "Something's wrong," she said.

Waro sniffed the air and growled.

"What is it?" Rithik said.

"Someone else is here," Waro said.

"Grimlocks," Laila said. "They don't usually—"

Then chaos broke loose around them.

One of the hunters screamed, and strange shouts and high-pitched shrieks erupted from the darkness. There were people ... or monsters ... all around them.

Rithik drew his sword with one hand and switched on his torch with the other. Darkness be damned!

The shock of sight was disorienting. The image he had of the cavern, the hunters, were all slightly different now that he could see them. And they were being attacked by something for which he had no image until he saw them in the light of his lantern.

Naked, hairless, human-like creatures, with translucent skin, eyeless faces, and large mouths fanged and gaping, swarmed around them. Their long bony fingers were tipped with sharp claws.

In a flash he saw the hunters locked in hand-to-hand combat. One hunter was down and was being hauled off by one of the monsters, while the others continued fighting.

One of the monsters leapt at him from the rocks above. Waro tackled the creature, toppling it over.

Another charged toward them in a frenzy, but Rithik cut the creature down with a slash of his sword.

There was a shriek from above.

Rithik looked up in time to see a huge, hairy, bat-like thing swoop out of the darkness, all claws and rows of sharp teeth, beady eyes, and twelve-foot leathery wings outstretched.

Gharbat, Rithik thought. He grabbed Laila and dragged her down to the ground. They hit hard on the rocks, and the gharbat swooped past where their heads had been. It continued on, grabbed one of the hairless man-things, and carried it off into the darkness, beating its enormous wings.

Within seconds the fight was over. The remaining creatures disappeared into the darkness beyond Rithik's light, and they were left in sudden silence to take stock of the dead and wounded.

Laila looked down at one of the dead creatures and finished her thought. "They don't usually come up this far."

There were three dead grimlocks. One hunter was missing. One was wounded. The two remaining hunters shielded their eyes from Rithik's light.

Waro ran around sniffing the air and guarding the perimeter.

Rithik turned the torch on low and hid it inside his vest so it glowed dimly through the fabric. He was reluctant to turn it off until he knew they were out of danger.

Laila examined the wounded hunter. He had an injured leg and multiple lacerations to the face and arms. "Nothing life threatening," Laila said, "just a sprained ankle."

"Eck is gone," The hunter said. It was Kethan's voice.

"Shouldn't we go after him?" Rithik said. "I'll bet Waro can track those things."

"It's no use," Kethan said. "He was dead before they hauled him off. And even if you did find the grimlocks, there would be nothing left of Eck when you did."

Laila busied herself bandaging Kethan's wounds. "You and Hanlo should return to the dwellings," she said.

"We can't leave you," Hanlo said.

"The grimlocks will return to their lairs below. You will slow us down more than Rithik now. The Halls of Maitreyu are not far off, and there you can follow us no further anyway."

They could not argue with the Moth Maram's decision, and after some protest they agreed to go back, promising to send other hunters to safeguard their return.

They watched the two hunters hobble off into the dark, back toward the dwellings, and they hurried on, moving quickly now that Rithik had a shred of light to see by.

At the end of the long chamber, Laila led them down into an insignificant looking crevice in the side wall. Through the narrow crack, a passage widened, spiraled right, dropped down, and opened up into a shockingly square room, with perfectly smooth walls that gleamed like black crystal. On the far side of the room was a pair of golden doors, etched with abstract rectilinear patterns.

"What is this place?"

"We know not. Maitreyu was here long before the people settled in the dwellings. And surely he will be here long after we are gone."

It did not look like the work of the ancients. This was unlike anything Rithik had seen before in any ruin or artifact.

For a moment, Rithik saw blue lights dancing beneath the glass-like surface of the crystal walls. They merged into patterns, shot upwards, and disappeared into the ceiling.

The golden doors slid open silently, and inside was a tubular chamber filled with soft blue light.

Laila beckoned him into the chamber. "Step into the light, and prepare for wonders never dreamt of."

19

CITY OF CRYSTAL

Rithik was past any pretense of caution. He trusted Laila. There was nothing else to do but take a breath and step through the golden doors. The soft blue light surrounded him in the small tubular room. Laila and Waro looked in on him.

"What now?" he said. There was no passage, and no other exit from the room.

"Wait a moment," Laila said. "And don't worry, we'll be right after you."

Don't worry? Rithik thought, wondering what he should be worrying about.

The floor beneath him vanished. But he did not fall so much as drop, slowly at first, and then more rapidly. It was uncanny, disconcerting, but he was not afraid, for although there was nothing around him, he felt held by some unseen force. Faster and faster he went, through a smooth-bored tube that rushed by. Impulsively he stuck out a hand to brush the wall, but he could not touch it. His hand seemed to slide along a cushion of air that he could not penetrate, no matter how hard he pushed.

The passage descended vertically, but curved this way and that, carrying Rithik effortlessly through what must have been a mile or more of solid rock.

Only when he dropped out of the tunnel into open space did he feel afraid, for it seemed then he was falling, high above the floor of a cavern hundreds of times larger than anything he had seen before, larger in fact than any enclosed space he had ever thought possible.

But he was still held by the same unseen force, as if being guided through an invisible tube of soft air. Below him, filling the vast cavern, were crystal towers as smooth as glass. And beneath the flat translucent surfaces of the buildings, if that's what they were, mesmerizing arrays of colored lights danced about like fireflies.

The tube of air in which he travelled curved gently until he was flying horizontally through the vast cavern. Looking back and up to where he had come from, he saw Waro drop out of a circular hole in the stone vault. His four legs and tail flailed in the air and Rithik could hear him howling.

A moment later Laila dropped out, soaring down through the air as if it were natural to her. As graceful as any bird, as majestic as the great eagle Samsa, she descended behind Rithik and Waro into the crystal city.

Rithik flailed his arms, managed to turn over in the air, and looked down. They flew over a glass-smooth road streaked with flares of light. As they continued on, the road merged and diverged, labyrinth like, growing into larger streets and boulevards. They gradually descended, eventually converging on a wide central highway that ran through the center of city. There, the invisible air tube set them down gently on the level ground.

Beneath their feet, light streaked to and from the flat façade of a huge building that filled one end of the vast cavern. The myriad smaller towers of the city rose around them.

"Where are we?" Waro said, craning his neck around to look at their strange surroundings.

Rithik felt disoriented … almost dizzy. The ghost flesh itched at the base of his neck, under his arm, and along the side of his ribs. Was this the spirit realm? Would he find Yananna here among the spirits? She alone could spare him. She alone could answer the questions he could not frame, and satisfy the longing he still felt in his heart.

"These are the halls of the great Maitreyu," Laila said. "Ahead lies the temple where you shall meet him."

In the distance Rithik saw a figure walking toward them. It shocked him back to his senses, and he half reached for the handle of his sword.

"It's all right," Laila said. "They are servants of Maitreyu."

As the figure approached, Rithik could see that although it appeared human in shape, there was something inhuman about it. The form was too general, too idealized. The gait was too unhindered by injury or age. The countenance was too free from excesses of thought or personality. As it got closer, Rithik saw it wore no clothes and had no sign of biological sex. Its skin appeared to be panels and wrappings of translucent plastic. Its joints were metallic, its muscles a kind of glowing blue material, shimmering with white light. It was, in short, a kind of mechanism.

Rithik had seen the shells of ancient robots in the markets of Pithtek when he was younger, but this was something way more advanced. This whole city, in fact, seemed like a mechanism on an entirely different level than anything the ancients had ever built.

The robot stopped in front of them and bowed in greeting. Its face was human but immobile, like a mask. The features were androgynous, and when it spoke the voice was neither masculine nor feminine. "Welcome. Please follow me. Maitreyu is expecting you."

"What is this place?" Rithik said.

"Come," said the robot, "Maitreyu will answer all questions."

The robot turned, and led them down the broad light-streaked highway, toward the huge building at the end of the vast cavern. When they were closer, Rithik could see that while this building was made of the same black, glass-like substance, its surface was inlaid with intricate gold patterns. Long lines converged on central golden doors at least a hundred feet high.

As the robot led them on, the huge golden doors swung inward slowly and silently. Inside was a massive hall, its sides lined with rectangular golden columns reaching up to the high flat ceiling. In front of every column stood an identical robot, and each one bowed as they passed. At the far end of the hall, a circular golden door opened like the dilating iris of a human eye.

The robot stepped to the side and beckoned them to continue through the round doorway.

Laila led them through. Waro followed. And finally Rithik stepped across the threshold of the portal. They stood at one end of another large rectangular hall. Although this room was slightly smaller than the preceding one, it was still at least a hundred feet high, a hundred feet long, and sixty feet wide.

At the far side of the hall was a solid golden wall covered in relief carvings. High on the wall a pair of piercing eyes gazed down at them, the pupils inlaid with the same black crystalline stone everything else was made of. Centered above those eyes was a third eye, set vertically. And carved into the gold, what looked like beams of light radiated from the third eye, a sunburst pattern stretching to every edge and corner of the wall.

A voice emanated from all around them. Like the voice of the robot, it was an androgynous voice, but louder, and somehow more intelligent, vastly intelligent, and full of strange and inexplicable power.

"Come forward and fear not. You are welcome in the halls of Maitreyu, Laila of the people, Waro the wanderer, and Rithik the hunter."

20

THE VOICE OF MAITREYU

The voice echoed through the great hall, and it beckoned them forward.

Rithik instinctively looked around, searching for some person, even another robot, from which the voice had come. But there was no other person or robot, just a huge hall, and a golden wall with three eyes staring down at them.

They followed Laila as she advanced to within a stone's throw of the golden wall. Rithik gazed up at the three enigmatic eyes, high on the wall, and the radiant sunburst that spread across its golden surface.

Laila addressed the wall, raising her voice in a gesture of grandeur. "Great Maitreyu, the elders of the people seek your guidance in the matter of these two outsiders, who have recently come to the realm of the dwellings. Some say they should be banished. Others to give them a place, though far from the spring."

"Let those who would stay live in peace among you. Give them a place near the spring, so that your actions reflect the kindness in the hearts of the people, and not the fears they hold."

"Your wisdom guides the people," Laila said. In the silence that followed, she added, "The elders wish to know, will others come from the outside world?"

"Worry not whether the dwellings will abide unchanged through the waking or ten-thousand wakings. All things in time come to an end. Let this not trouble you. Cling not to an illusion of the future. It is only a projection of your hopes and fears. This moment now is all there is."

"Your wisdom guides us," Laila said, and she bowed.

Silence once again filled the great hall.

Maybe it was his imagination, or the giant eyes staring down at him from the golden wall, but Rithik felt an unmistakable presence in that silence, a far-reaching consciousness, ready to respond to the slightest thought or word or movement. It felt like the surface of a vast still ocean waiting for a stone to be dropped in.

Laila turned to them. "Ask a question and Maitreyu will answer."

"I have a question," Waro said. "I have wandered dhrough many ruins, but I have never seen a place like dhis. Who built it, and who are you who dwells here?"

"The civilizations of humanity and the orders of machines have risen and fallen throughout the ages. I am but a remnant of a bygone age, long forgotten, and yet, from the first unto the last, I am."

Thunderous silence followed Maitreyu's pronouncement.

"Well, dhat clears dhat up," Waro muttered.

Rithik's mind raced. Was this voice, this being, some kind of artifact from a civilization even older than the ancients? Was it a spirit, transcending all of human history? Was it something else? Was this whole city some kind of giant mechanical mind?

"How is it that you knew our names?" Rithik said, emboldened to ask it a question.

"I know them as I know you are standing here before me. All phenomena are transparent."

"Is this then the realm of spirits?" Rithik asked.

"To answer no would be a lie, but to answer yes would surely mislead you. This is what is. It is simply thus. Everything else is only an idea. Matter and spirit, body and mind, life and death, these are only concepts you still cling to."

"I don't understand."

"Let go of yourself, Rithik, hunter of Tavala, and the truth will be revealed to you."

The ghost flesh crawled beneath the skin of his neck and chest. It would kill him, and yet how could he let go of himself? How could he stop searching? How could he give up?

"I am infected with ghost flesh," Rithik said. "Is there no cure, no hope to be found in any realm?"

"There can be no escape from yourself. Whether you live or die makes no difference once you have seen your true nature."

Something stirred in Rithik, something deep in the back of his mind, but its approach felt like death, like annihilation, or madness. And every thought he had, every feeling, was to look away and hold fast to this life with every ounce of strength and resolve he had.

"Free yourself of everything," Maitreyu said.

Despite himself, Rithik heard in this voice something he could not explain in the context of any artifact or machine he had ever encountered.

Love.

Tears came to Rithik's eyes. "I just … I can't let go."

"Then your search is not yet over. You must continue on until your journey ends. There is no other way."

"I came in search of Yananna's cave, but have not found it. How am I to go on? Where am I to go?"

"I will show you a path. There you must continue your journey. To the very end you alone must go."

Suddenly, the golden wall and the eyes of Maitreyu vanished. His friends and the very hall they stood in disappeared. A vast emptiness expanded around him, and in a flash this emptiness filled with a vision of the lower caverns. He saw in all directions simultaneously, but he felt no sense of disorientation, either by this fact or by the maze of caverns surrounding him. He knew exactly where he was, not far from where the grimlocks had attacked their party.

His awareness began to move through the cavern as if by will alone, and yet he could not discern whether this will came from within or without. Disembodied, he floated up and over a ridge, down into a depression, and across a field of rubble. As he went, the movement itself imprinted an indelible map upon his mind. He entered a small side passage and proceeded through a series of twisting, branching tunnels to arrive at a small, natural chamber.

In the middle of the chamber the floor had collapsed into a vertical shaft, perfectly cylindrical, descending into a darkness his vision could not penetrate. And there, attached to the side of the shaft, was a metal ladder.

He heard Maitreyu's voice. "Here is your path. You will know when you have found its end, but do not stop until you have reached it."

Rithik felt an irresistible draw, a compulsion to descend the ladder, to follow the path the Maitreyu had shown him. He had found his way once more, and he knew he could do nothing but go on. Perhaps he did not understand it, but he would continue searching, and he would follow this path to whatever end.

Then, just as suddenly as he had been transported into this vision, he was back in the great hall, the golden wall and the eyes of Maitreyu staring down at him.

He looked down at Waro and over at Laila, and realized that no time had passed. The course of his vision had been instantaneous.

"Are you all right?" Waro said.

Rithik nodded. "I know now where I must go. We have to return to the lower caves."

Laila held her gaze fixed on the golden wall, awaiting any further words of wisdom or instruction, but Maitreyu had fallen silent. The great machine mind, if that was indeed what it was in any meaningful way, had gone on to other matters, other realms, other dreams. And at last, with some hesitation to leave such a wondrous place, they departed the halls of Maitreyu. They were carried through the air once more by invisible forces and returned to the small room from whence they had come.

21

RITHIK'S PATH

When they arrived back at the site of the grimlock ambush, Rithik shined his light around the area. It was the right place. He spotted some dark bloodstains on the ground. But the bodies of the dead grimlocks were gone. Beyond, off in a direction they had not traveled, Rithik could see the way Maitreyu had shown him. The ghost flesh itched at the back of his neck, crawling across his chest, and he felt no less sure of his path. He had to go on.

"I must part with you both," Rithik said, "and go alone on my way."

"Why must you go?" Laila said.

"The ghost flesh will take me soon."

"There is a place for both of you near the spring in the dwellings. Life is good there, however long it lasts."

"I must keep searching," Rithik said. "Maitreyu has shown me where I must go."

Laila sighed. Right or wrong, she could bear no argument against the wisdom of Maitreyu.

And right or wrong, Rithik felt he must go on, even if it meant he would meet death alone in some unknown labyrinth deep beneath the surface of the earth. If that was what he was meant to find, he would find it.

"You sure you know what you're doing?" Waro said.

Rithik nodded.

Waro huffed.

"What will you do?" Rithik said.

"Maybe someday I'll find my way back to dhe surface," Waro said, "but for now I'll take a break from wandering, and live for a while among dhe people. It's as good a place as any."

Rithik nodded.

Laila looked up and he met her large eyes in the torchlight.

"No long goodbyes," Rithik said. "I've known you both only a short time … and yet … I'm sad to leave you. Take care of yourselves, and each other."

Waro gave a brief singular nod, and wagged his tail.

Laila's gaze locked on Rithik. She seemed about to speak, as if she were struggling to form the words in her mind.

"So long," Rithik said. Preempting any further good-bye, he turned and walked away without another word.

He went up over the ridgeline, down into a depression, and out of sight from his friends.

As when he went out beyond the pale of Tavala, out into the wilderness, he did not look back. He could not afford to doubt his actions then, and he could not afford it now.

He crossed a large field of scattered rock as he headed perpendicular to the long axis of the huge cavern. He walked for a while, and though in his mind he was sure of his direction, the way seemed longer than in his vision. Of course, that made sense, when he had to walk instead of float or fly, and when the very space through which he traveled seemed more real and inflexible.

Slowly, however, he made his way toward the side of the cavern. The ceiling got lower, and the drooping stalactites drew closer and closer, until they were almost within reach. And there, beyond a column of rock, in the side wall of the cavern, he located the small side passage he had seen in his vision. He had to climb down into it, squeezing through an opening barely wider than his shoulders.

Inside, the passage opened up a bit, and he was able to move forward, half stooped to keep from hitting his head on the jagged rock a few inches above him. Steadfastly he proceeded forward through a series of turns and a multitude of branching tunnels, without ever losing the feeling that he knew exactly where he was going.

At last he arrived at the chamber from his vision. It was real. Just as Maitreyu had shown him. In the middle of the natural room the floor was collapsed, and in the hole was a cylindrical shaft, cut through the rock, descending into the darkness beyond his torch light. Attached to the side of the shaft was a metal ladder.

Rithik checked all his gear. His sword and knife, his chatter box, his torch, his pistol, and his last grenade were all secure. Inside his pack he had a water bottle, a few meager rations, his old repair kit, and a few odds and ends. He sat down, put his legs over the edge, and dropped a small stone down the shaft. He heard it clatter off the ladder once or twice, then nothing. Then maybe he heard it hit bottom, but he couldn't be sure.

Maitreyu's voice was still fresh in his memory though. "Here is your path." The voice echoed through the chambers of Rithik's mind.

He reached down to grab the top of the ladder. With a good grip, he swung a leg around to catch a rung with his boot. A few careful steps down and he was descending the ladder comfortably, one rung at a time.

Soon the bubble of light from his torch, secure in its mesh pocket, couldn't reach the shaft opening and the room above. Looking up, Rithik saw only the ladder, the smooth walls of the vertical shaft, and darkness beyond. Looking down, it was the same. He could not know how far the ladder descended. Already his hands ached, and his feet had almost slipped twice on the smooth rungs.

Foot and hand, foot and hand, he descended into the darkness. He wished he had put a few stones in his pocket to drop on the way down, but it was too late. There was nothing to do but keep going, and so he did, descending ever deeper into the awaiting darkness.

At last he glanced down to see the end of the cylindrical shaft. The ladder appeared to extend down farther. A few more steps and he saw a flat floor below. The shaft opened up and Rithik descended into a cubical room cut out of solid rock. The ladder reached down below the ceiling to within a few feet of the floor, where Rithik hopped off and stretched his cramped limbs.

He looked around. The room was about a fifteen-foot cubical space. In addition to the cylindrical shaft above, centered on each wall was an identical cylindrical passage, the same diameter as the shaft, but of course without the ladder.

Great. Which way now? Maitreyu had given him no further instructions. Continue your search. This is your path. Go alone to the very end. You will know when you reach it. That was the whole of the machine-god's instructions.

Just like that he was on his own again. He flicked the switch on his chatter box and walked around the room holding it out at each passage. Nothing. And even with his light on high, he could see nothing but tunnel down each one. Nor could he hear or smell anything, or feel any trace of a breeze or change in temperature. Nothing that would even hint at which way to go.

Did it matter? He didn't even really know what he was looking for anymore. Was it Yananna's cave? Was it salvation? Was it an answer to a question he had not yet formed? Or was it something else?

The only asymmetries in the entire situation was the position of the ladder on one side of shaft above, and the absence of a shaft below. Could it mean something? Surely not. Even if it did, it didn't tell him anything. Could it mean follow the tunnel in the direction of the ladder, or the opposite, or one of the sides? No, it meant nothing.

Rithik turned around looking at each passage. How would he choose? He found himself wondering how he chose anything. He had not chosen to be born. He knew that. Had he chosen to be hunter of Tavala? Had he chosen to leave Elaya? He didn't know. Had he chosen to risk the city of dust or to venture into the Western Desert? Had he chosen to enter the cave or to descend into this labyrinth? At the time it had all seemed like what he must do. There was always something that tipped the scales. But was it him? Was it even possible not to have done the things he had done?

Certainly not now.

He supposed he could go back. Was that the real choice he had, to go back or go forward? If that was the case, he knew already he would go forward. That decision was already made. But which way? Functionally it made no difference with the information he had. He could think about it for a few minutes or an hour or five hours, but eventually he would just go down one of the tunnels. They had eaten the last of the canned food in the lower caves, and the longer he thought, the quicker his meager rations of ubok would run out.

It did not feel like a choice, but he chose one of the tunnels, the one to his right, and walked down it. He supposed he could always backtrack, but somehow, deep down, he knew that wouldn't really be an option.

22

MAZE OF THE MIND

Rithik counted paces: eighty-six, eight-seven, eighty-eight, and so on. The cylindrical tunnel went straight. His footsteps echoed through the interior. At one hundred and eleven paces he reached another cubical room.

There was no ladder or shaft overhead, and it only had two other passages, one going straight, and another left. But otherwise it was exactly the same as the previous room, same size, same cubical shape.

On an impulse, Rithik went left and continued on his way. He supposed he didn't want to feel a hundred percent bound to his choice of direction in the previous room, so by going left he mitigated his commitment.

Eager to see where this tunnel would lead, he forgot about counting his paces. But soon enough he reached another cubical room. This one had a tunnel going in each direction, and in the middle of the room, a shaft going down, complete with a metal ladder like the one he had descended before.

He glanced down the shaft, but he didn't like the idea of going farther down, so this time he went right … or was it left? By the next room he couldn't remember.

This room had passages going left, right, and down. He went right.

Mid-passage, Rithik thought maybe he should have been marking his way somehow, but it was too late. He was lost again, in this maze of strange tunnels. Maybe he had been lost his whole life. Maybe at some point when he was still young, he went left when he should have gone right, and he'd been lost ever since.

The next room went straight, left, and down. He went straight.

What *were* these tunnels anyway? What could such tunnels and rooms be used for? And who built them? Were they mining tunnels? Air ducts? They seemed to go on and on without end.

The next room again had passages in all directions and down. That was three or four rooms with a down ladder. Perhaps, Rithik thought, he *should* go down. Maybe the real path was down. Maybe whatever he was looking for was down there somewhere. It was something anyway.

Rithik glanced down the shaft. In the light of his torch he could see another room through a mere five feet of vertical shaft. He mounted the ladder and climbed down.

The room below had passages in every direction. He tried to orient himself, hoping to continue in the direction he had been going above. But he wasn't sure. He'd gotten distracted when he decided to go down and descended the ladder, and now he felt all turned around. With the exception of the passages, every room looked the same in every direction. It was maddening.

He paused and took off his pack. He took a sip of water from his water bottle and indulged in a bite of dried ubok. There wasn't much left. He wrapped the remaining meat up and stuffed it into one of his vest pockets. Ubok, he thought. So far from the surface, in this insane place, uboks didn't even seem real. That meat was the only indication they ever existed.

He chose a tunnel by simply walking down the one he was already facing. What difference could it make? He was lost already. But when he came across another shaft leading down, he went back to his previous thought and took it. And so he proceeded, but after a few more rooms he began to have doubts about the down idea.

In the next room he went up. But as he climbed up and out of the shaft, he thought maybe changing his mind was a mistake. If he kept changing his mind, his thoughts could drive him round and round in circles forever. He remembered what Waro had said about finding the way out of a labyrinth. Pick a direction and then always go right … or left? No, it didn't matter. He would go right. Always right.

It was just another thought, but at least it was a logical one. And if he stuck with it he would have a method for getting out of here.

Of course the next room had only a left turn available to him. In this case that counts as straight he thought, and tried not to confuse himself by thinking about it further. He just went left and pressed on. But the very next room presented him with another left passage and a passage up, and he had to think again. Was left or up straight in this case?

He stopped to think about it. He yawned and rubbed his eyes. He realized he hadn't slept in a long while. He felt tired but willed himself to think and press on. Now, he thought, left or up shouldn't matter. Right? But he had to be consistent. What he needed was to set down a list of priorities and keep it straight. So what was better, left or up? Or down? He had to consider that now since it was sure to come up sooner or later.

So what he would do is this. If he couldn't go right he would go straight. If he couldn't go straight he would go left. If he couldn't go any of those directions … what was better, up or down? This was the same trouble he had at the beginning. There was no way to really know. At the start he had gone down though, and he had been sure that had been his path. That was the last time he felt sure of anything. Everything after that had been guesswork. For all he knew these rooms were rearranging themselves when he wasn't looking.

That was a crazy thought. Where did it come from? How strange was it that he could think a thought and think it crazy all in the same moment? Where were any of these thoughts coming from? How astonishing that he had never really considered it. Now it seemed there were two of him. Suddenly it seemed the thinker of his thoughts and the observer of his thoughts were separate selves. How was that possible? But these too were just thoughts.

In this direction lay madness, he thought. He had to focus, just focus on the task at hand.

Down.

He had started going down. If he couldn't go any horizontal direction other than the way he came, he would go down. And if he couldn't go any other direction other than the way he came, he would go up.

There, he thought. That's settled.

He mounted the ladder and climbed up twenty feet into the next room. Then he went right, and continued on his way.

After proceeding like this for some time he noticed something else. He was stooped over, neck and back arched, knees bent as he walked down a long tunnel. That had not always been the case. He remembered in earlier tunnels he had been able to stand upright, with the ceiling a few inches from his head.

When had that changed? He hadn't noticed. On the one hand, it was a change, which meant he was getting somewhere. Or did it? No, it meant he wasn't going in circles. At least it meant that. On the other hand, like every previous change, he had no way of knowing if it was good or bad. He couldn't know if it meant he was getting somewhere or nowhere.

When he got to the next room, Rithik examined all the tunnel entrances. They all seemed to be the same size. But somehow, somewhere along the way, they had gotten smaller. There was no right tunnel, so he went straight. In the next room, again, the tunnels seemed the same size. He went left, and then down, and then straight.

In the next room, again the entrances seemed the same size, but he could swear he had to stoop a little bit lower to enter them than he had several rooms ago. He went straight again.

This tunnel went on for a long ways. He walked on and on. How long had he been in this maze already? He had no idea. A day maybe. Maybe longer. What did a day even mean anymore? He walked so long that he started to count his paces again. After two hundred paces he stopped. He was bent over almost at the waist.

The tunnel was getting narrower. Soon he would have to get down on all fours. He wondered, should he go back?

Where would it get him? Back into the same maze he had come from, and soon he would have to eat the last of his food, drink the last of his water.

Breathe his last breath.

Think his last thought.

He continued forward, and in another hundred paces he got down on all fours and began to crawl.

For a long time he crawled, until his knees and the palms of his hands were bruised, battered, and aching with pain. Soon he could crawl only with his head down, and the top of the tunnel scraped across his back. In the darkness, from the light of his torch, he could see only a few feet ahead of him and nothing behind. It made no difference. For hours it seemed he had seen nothing but tunnel, and he had stopped wondering when it would end. He just kept crawling, through his pain, through the odor of his sweat, and through the expanding limits of his exhaustion.

He regretted not spending more time saying goodbye to Laila and Waro. He regretted not saying something more. But what would he have said, anyway?

He just crawled on. After some time—he had no idea how long—he paused in the cramped tunnel to drink the last of his water, and eat the last of his ubok. Right there, he left behind his pack, the empty water bottle, a sweater, his bedroll, and his old repair kit. He didn't think he'd be repairing anything anymore. Then he lay down and began to crawl forward on his belly.

Eventually it seemed like this was all there was, an endless tube of stone through which he wriggled like a snake. But ever forward he went, ever searching with his face two inches from ground. What would he find? What was there ever to find?

On and on he went, until he realized it was pitch dark. His torch had gone out. When had it happened? He didn't know. It had to have been only a moment ago. His view was so restricted already, and his mind so addled by fatigue and crawling that he hadn't noticed right away. But it must have been just a moment ago.

He rolled onto his side and groped around with his hands to check the torch. It was still in its mesh pocket and switched on. It should be working, unless that damn power cell had crapped out on him. It should have been good for years. These old torches were so reliable—some had been passed down for generations.

He turned the torch off and back on again.

Nothing.

He tried again.

Nothing.

Rithik took a breath, and tried one more time.

Complete and total darkness.

This change was dramatic. Although he had seen nothing but the stone floor of the tunnel for a long time, he couldn't see his hand right in front his face now. There was little chance of getting any more lost than he already was, and he could feel his way for now, but what would he do if he ever got out of this tunnel?

The thought was chilling, to wander in the darkness until one became mad, or died of thirst, or was taken by the ghost flesh … or something worse.

He had slowly gotten used to the narrow tunnel, the closeness of the walls, but now in the darkness the walls seemed to close in on him. He thought about the incredible mass of rock and dirt that lay above him, and it threatened to squeeze him right out of existence.

Rithik gasped and realized he had been holding his breath. He gulped air and tried to calm himself down. He was still in the same tunnel, and until he reached the end that was all he had to worry about.

He rolled back onto his belly. Slowly at first, he began to crawl forward again.

Like a worm he inched forward in the darkness. His legs twitched like foreign objects to push him, and his hands groped ahead like fleshy probes before pulling him another few inches.

He lost all sense of time and space. He imagined he saw flashes of light, shapes, faces in the darkness, but nothing lasted except the grim reality that lay before him, inch after inch, unto his death.

At last, he couldn't crawl any more. He didn't know if the tunnel had grown too narrow and wedged him in, or if he had simply stopped out of sheer exhaustion. It didn't matter. He was done.

In the pitch darkness he turned over on his back.

He thought about Laila and Waro. The truth was, he had never said a proper goodbye to anybody. Not to Elaya when he had gone north or when he had left Tavala. Not to Praya when he had gone on that spring expedition to the river city. Not to his father when his father had gone east. Not … oh Yananna … his mother!

She hadn't even recognized him. Had she?

Of course, she had never been the same after Praya's death. She forgot more and more. After a while she seemed to forget who Rithik was. Maybe he never admitted it, but he was hurt when this woman who had loved him, who had given birth to him and raised him from a baby, no longer seemed to know him, or even care. When he told her he had the ghost flesh she had no reaction. She just stared into empty space and said nothing.

But he remembered now, when he had left Tavala for good, old man Hargen had led her out to see him off. Rithik stood with one foot beyond the pale, hand resting on the high wooden gate, which was opened just enough to let him pass. His mother had met his eyes one last time.

Perhaps there had been a spark of recognition.

She seemed just about to say something, but Rithik didn't wait.

"So long," he said, and walked out into the wilderness.

Rithik's body convulsed. His chest tightened, like a red-hot iron had poked into him. And there in the darkness of the tunnel, he wept and wept, without a trace of shame, and without a shred of hope.

He forgot himself entirely. He wept until the tears stopped of their own accord. He wished he had said something to her. He wished he had said something to them all. But somehow it was all right. There was absolutely nothing he could do, and that was all right.

Things were the way they were.

He supposed he would sleep for a while. He would wake again probably, but he didn't know or care what would happen next. He would make no more choices, no more decisions. It was all a relief really, he thought, and he was just about to drift off when he saw a light.

23

CITY OF METAL

For a second, Rithik thought it must be the dim flashes and the phantasmagoria of images that are the prelude to dreams. Then he blinked his eyes in the darkness and felt quite sure he was awake. He felt the aching pain in his knees. He heard his own steady breathing. And he saw above him a dim blue light illuminating the smooth rock of the tunnel overhead.

The light changed, flickering red for a moment, and then greenish, yellow, white, and then blue again

He put a hand up in front of his face. Yes, that was real. He could see his hand. He wiggled his fingers and saw them wiggle right before his eyes. It seemed amazing to him, wondrous, but real.

Slowly, Rithik turned over onto his belly again in the narrow tunnel. He craned his head back and looked straight ahead.

Sure enough, there was a pinhole of light. He could not tell how far away. An opening? A room? The end of the tunnel? It was definitely something.

The light flickered again red, went through a series of colors, and back to blue again.

Rithik took a breath and stared at the light. He felt some of his energy return, and a growing desire to find out what that was.

He inched forward.

He reached ahead and pulled himself forward with hands and forearms. He wiggled his torso ahead, and pushed with his feet.

Oh, yes, this was familiar. He could do this a little more. He could go a little farther to see what he would find.

Every few minutes he looked up.

The light was getting larger. It seemed a kind of disk of light now, which continued to periodically shift in colors.

He still could not gauge the distance.

With increasing vigor he crawled forward. Gradually the light became brighter and brighter. More and more it reflected off the smooth sides of the tunnel.

The next time he looked up the light was even larger and seemed to have a grainy quality to it. He still couldn't tell what he was looking at. He felt as if his mind were playing tricks on him. There was a light. Of that, he was sure. But what was it? Was it a luminous wall at the end of the tunnel?

He put his head down and crawled.

Finally, he could see the tunnel ended. And it didn't seem far off. Whatever the light was, it was coming from beyond the tunnel itself.

He crawled forward as fast as he could.

Closer … closer.

At last he stuck his head out the end of the tunnel.

He beheld, not far off in the distance, across a field of scree and rubble that stretched out from the base of the slope below him, a giant, luminous sign on the side of an old building. It flickered with images and strange writing. It was the biggest screen Rithik had ever seen.

Chrome lizards danced around the edges of the screen, reflecting a dazzling blue light. They swirled inward in a kaleidoscopic frenzy and disappeared. A big word zoomed across the screen in strange red symbols. A woman's face stood out against a green field. She said something but there was no sound. Then, with delicate fingers she put something in her mouth and smiled. The image faded, and the chrome lizards began their dance again.

Rithik gazed in wonder with his head poked out the end of the long tunnel. It was another truly immense cavern. Tilted towers of metal and glass scraped the cavern's jagged stone ceiling. Crumbling ruins stood, half toppled into the remains of prehistoric roads. Whole walls were plastered with giant screens that came to life, flickering with an endless barrage of colorful images and indecipherable words. Lights twinkled on tower spires, and blinked on inside a few random empty windows.

The fragments of half a city were here. This was no city of the ancients though. There were no elegant ceramite structures with their rounded organic shapes. There were no flitter cars or landing parks. This was something stranger, and perhaps older than any ruin on the surface. But neither was it the cold inhuman artifact that he had seen in the halls of Maitreyu. This was a human city, but unlike any he had ever seen before.

As if to prove the point, the first thing Rithik grabbed as he dragged himself out of the tunnel turned out to be a human skull. Rithik tossed it aside, where it clattered among the rocks, and wriggled his legs out of the narrow tunnel with relief. He stood up with difficulty, stretched his battered limbs, and stared with wonder at the lost city.

It appeared only a portion of the city remained, somehow trapped here, buried and forgotten in ages past. Its edges dwindled into half-ruined buildings. Its roads disappeared into rubble fields, flowstone, and the sloping hills that reached up to the cavern walls.

Rithik checked his remaining gear. His torch still didn't work, but there was plenty of light here. And that meant power. For a moment he reckoned on searching for a power cell, but finding one wasn't likely. Cell compatibility was an issue even among the artifacts left behind by the ancients. He couldn't expect compatibility across civilizations from different ages lost in time.

Rithik descended a slope littered with human bones. He headed toward a road by the giant screen, which led inward to the middle of the clustered buildings. Once again, he set off on a search. He really didn't know what he was searching for, but the impulse was strong from a lifetime of hunting.

When Rithik reached the crumbling road, he checked his weapons once more. He didn't expect there'd be tokmen here, but he supposed there could be grimlocks, gharbats, or something worse. After spending most of his life hunting among the ruins of the ancients, this place was disorienting and strange with its flat-sided towers and its grid-patterned streets. It was nothing like the radiating boulevards of the ancient cities. Where was its center? There was no way to know.

He gazed up at the giant flashing screens on the buildings as he walked along abandoned streets. He tried to make sense of the strange, urgent words, but he couldn't read them. Guessing by their context they seemed to say things like *buy*, *eat*, *beautiful*, *desire*, *desire*, *desire*, but he had no way to know. He ambled on, intoxicated by the colored lights that flashed across the broken concrete.

He reached an intersection where the road he traveled crossed a wide boulevard. Here and there the buildings showed their metal skeletons where their faces had eroded, shattered, or crumbled off.

Something moved in the shadowy entrance of a nearby building. Rithik's hand found the hilt of his sword and he crouched slightly, waiting, watching to see what might emerge.

A four-legged figure shambled out, limping on one hind leg. Was it a goat? A dog? It came toward him, headless, and as it neared, Rithik realized it was some kind of robot. It limped forward with a strangely animal-like gait. It didn't look dangerous. It appeared to have a tray held steady by some mechanism on its back. On the tray were an array of cups and glasses.

The thing stopped a few feet from Rithik, the whirring of its limb servos suddenly quiet. It made a soft *boop* noise and the tray on its back rose up. It said something, the artificial voice emanating from an array of instruments where its head should have been. The glasses were empty, so although Rithik was thirsty, he ignored the offer.

Another robot emerged from the shadows. This one was human shaped, but only crudely resembled a person. Its limbs were cylindrical tubes with metal mechanical joints, poorly articulated. It had a stilted, waddling, artificial gait. Its face was an oval screen, upon which was the face of a strange-looking man. He smiled and appeared to speak, but no sound emerged from the robot. It approached and started pointing in different directions.

Another robot appeared, and another. One was a can thing on wheels with ambulatory hoses. The other was a humanoid torso dragging itself into the street with a single arm. Its other arm and legs were missing. Its screen-face grimaced as if acting out the effort. They both came toward him. As they neared the humanoid robot shouted, "Hora! Hora!"

Rithik wasn't sure what to do.

Soon there was a crowd of robots approaching from every direction. They were all shapes and sizes, and in every possible state of disrepair. Some looked cobbled together by other robots from a hodgepodge of spare parts and models. They walked and rolled, lurched and shook. They whirred and beeped. They shouted and spoke, but all in a language Rithik could not fathom.

They seemed to want to help. They seemed to want to serve him in some way or other. They jostled for position as they got closer, pressing in on him, a cacophonous hoard of metal mutants.

Rithik turned around looking for a path through them, but he was already surrounded. He was trapped by their insufferable servitude.

"Back off," Rithik shouted. "Go away! I don't want anything!"

But they did not heed his words, or more likely, did not understand them.

More and more robots joined the crowd. Some pushed forward and climbed over others to reach him. The mass of machines surged closer and closer, threatening to crush him. Some had shreds of rubbery skin and articulated faces, contorting into nightmares, with missing eyes or ears or jaws. The closest ones were all shouting and talking at once, a maddening gibberish of unintelligible offers. They would pile on top of him. They would tear him apart.

A robot behind him put a cold metallic hand on his shoulder.

He brushed it off, whirling around.

"Get back!" he shouted, pushing the robot away and drawing his sword in the space he created.

But they would not retreat.

Just when he thought he would have to act, there was a terrible, grinding metallic sound in the distance.

All the robots stopped, were silent for a second. Then they all seemed to talk amongst themselves.

They began to back up.

There was another sound, another metallic screech and then a crumbling crash of rock and debris.

The mass of robots panicked and scattered. They turned and lurched off. They ran if they could. They tripped over each other. They disappeared in the shadows. They fled into buildings. They vanished out of sight. He saw a small three-legged thing hop into a pile of scrap metal, and they were gone, every last one of them. The streets were as abandoned as they had been minutes ago.

Only there was that sound: a metallic screech and then a crushing thud.

Reeah pkhhsh, reeah pkhhsh, reeah pkhhsh.

It sounded like footsteps. Really big footsteps.

He stared down the boulevard in the direction of the noise. Colored lights flickered across the abandoned street.

Reeah pkhhsh, reeah pkhhsh, reeah pkhhsh.

It was getting louder.

He thought about running, but he didn't know what he was running from, and besides—

A giant hulking robot stomped into the boulevard from behind one of the buildings, and in a fraction of a second Rithik took it in.

It was at least twenty feet tall. Each huge armored iron leg seemed to crater the concrete beneath its feet. The upper body was a bulky mass of dirty, battle-scarred armor plating. A gun barrel protruded from one side of the chest, swiveling around as if looking for targets. A metallic skull-like head gazed out from a hooded enclosure. Its red eyes scanned the street. One arm was a huge gun with six barrels. The other was some kind of giant cannon with a smaller barrel beneath it. On its shoulders were metal spikes, upon which had been skewered human skulls.

There wasn't a shred of doubt as to the purpose of this thing. It was a machine designed to exterminate human life. Nor was there any doubt that Rithik was any match for it.

24

The Weapons of War

The robot's big multi-barreled gun arm turned to bear, and Rithik ran for the entryway of the nearest building.

The world seemed to explode around him. He dove through the open doorway and skidded across the floor, as a storm of metal chewed up the stone entryway, sending a stream of debris scattering in after him.

The firing stopped, and Rithik rolled up to his feet and kept moving. A few small service robots scattered out of his way.

His ears were ringing, but somehow he heard the thing coming.

Reeah pkhhsh, reeah pkhhsh, reeah pkhhsh.

He scrambled up a nearby stairway as the lobby filled with a jet of liquid fire.

Searing heat and black smoke chased him up the stairs, grabbing at his back and neck as he ran.

Reeah pkhhsh, reeah pkhhsh. Zhzzz, zhzzz.

Rithik reached the top of the stairs, burst through a door and ran straight. He had no idea what he was doing, or what his plan was. That thing was hunting him! And he was just desperate to keep doing something, keep moving, keep surviving. But how could he stop such a monster?

An open window loomed before him. Below he could see the war machine, crouched, and peering into the entryway of the building.

Rithik pulled his last grenade, maybe his last chance, from his belt.

He pulled the pin, waited a second, and tossed it down where it clattered to a stop at the robot's feet. The thing looked down to see what it was, and the grenade exploded in a ball of fire and smoke and shrapnel.

The robot staggered backward, but when the smoke cleared it stood straight and looked up. Rithik stared into its glowing red eyes, and if the angry metal skull face could look any angrier, it did now. The big cannon arm arced upward.

Rithik turned and ran toward the back of the building. A moment later the room behind him exploded, shaking the entire building, pelting Rithik with debris, and sending him spiraling to the floor in the concussive shockwave.

The world went silent. He may have blacked out for a moment. Then he writhed in pain and confusion on the ground. His whole being hurt, as if he had been torn apart and put back together. He struggled to understand what his arms and legs were doing, and to reassert some conscious control over them.

He crawled forward. His sword was gone. Another explosion rocked the building behind him. Debris fell from the ceiling around him. Another explosion went off. The building shifted beneath Rithik. The room filled with smoke and dust.

Rithik pulled himself to his feet. He could hardly see anything. He knew he had to move, had to get out. He staggered forward. Another explosion knocked him to his knees for a moment, but he got up and moved on.

Part of the building behind him collapsed, and it felt like the whole thing could cave in at any minute.

He staggered forward. Where were the stairs? Didn't matter. He had to keep moving.

He came to an open window on the back side of the building. He was only one story up, maybe a little less because of a slope in the road. He jumped, just as another explosion rocked the building behind him.

He hit the pavement hard, collapsed both legs and rolled over his shoulder. Might have hurt his ankle, didn't know, didn't matter. The way ahead opened up onto a field of rubble. He stood up and started running, best he could.

Multiple explosions went off in the building behind him. He glanced back and saw the whole structure began to collapse like a house of cards. A tremendous noise seemed to shake the entire cavern.

Within seconds an expanding cloud of dust enveloped him. Another few steps and his ankle gave way. He collapsed to the ground, coughing and gasping for breath. And there he lay until the larger debris settled and some of the dust began to clear.

He turned on his side, sat up and looked back at the giant pile of rubble and twisted metal the building had become. Still flashing screens beyond the building's remains lit up the lingering dust cloud in an ever-changing array of colored lights.

Was it over? Had the robot been crushed in the collapse? Rithik had barely formed the thought when something moved. A heap of debris bulged up and fell off the rising silhouette of the death machine. Its red eyes scanned the ground ahead.

Rithik held still, but a moment later the giant robot began to stomp through the rubble and debris. It headed straight towards him. *Reeah pkhhsh, reeah pkhhsh.*

Rithik scrambled backward, tried to get up, collapsed again, and saw doom come stomping toward him. There was nowhere to run. He was in the middle of open ground. The nearest buildings were back the other way, and the rubble field extended to a steep embankment.

He pulled the pistol from his vest pocket, took aim, squeezed the trigger and fired off a round. He must have missed. He fired again and again. One bolt ricocheted uselessly off the robot's armor, and then the pistol was empty.

Reeah pkhhsh, reeah pkhhsh.

This was it then. He would die here. Not by the ghost flesh, but as the last casualty of a prehistoric war.

Reeah pkhhsh, reeah pkhhsh. Any second the monster would open fire.

From behind him, a single beam of orange light blasted over Rithik's head and blew off the robot's big gun arm. A second blast hit it in the leg.

What? Rithik looked back, up the embankment to where the beam had originated. He saw Laila standing there with a smoking Mark IV laser half as big as she was. She took aim once more, and orange fire erupted from the barrel of the laser.

The blast hit the robot dead center, piercing the armor in a firestorm of molten metal. Its innards exploded. For a moment afterwards it stood, as if it might still take a step, but then it teetered forward and fell face first into the rubble.

Rithik heard Waro's howl and looked back to see the dog's head pop up over the edge of the embankment.

Laila lowered the Mark IV and let it hang from its sling, smoke still trickling out of the barrel.

Rithik laughed. Overwhelmed with relief he laughed. Filled with joy to see his friends, he laughed and laughed.

Laila and Waro made their way down the embankment and across the rubble field to where Rithik sat. Waro ran to him, barking with excitement. He jumped onto Rithik, rolled over on his back, then sprang up and ran around him barking.

"All right, all right," Rithik said.

Finally Waro stopped and sat down, but he couldn't help letting out another few barks.

"All right," Rithik said. "It's good to see you too."

"You look terrible," Laila said.

"It's just the light," Rithik said.

Laila laughed.

"Help me up," Rithik said. He tried not to put too much weight on his ankle as Laila pulled him to his feet.

He was coated in dust. His clothes were torn into rags. His hands were covered in blood and grime, and he imagined his face wasn't much better.

"How did you find me? Why?"

"I had a dream," Laila said. "I knew you were in trouble."

"But the maze?"

"The great Maitreyu guided us by a swifter route."

"It seems you took dhe long way," Waro said.

Rithik laughed. He had definitely taken the long way. But what matter now? It was the way he had taken. Perhaps somehow, it was the only way he could have taken. Perhaps it was the way he had needed.

25

THE CROSSING

Together, they made their way through the lost city, beneath the colored lights of flashing screens. Here and there, service robots peered out at them from buildings long devoid of human presence. But the machines only watched them pass, and did not come out. If they awaited some kind of salvation, or if they held out hope that the human citizens of this forgotten city would return, they would go on waiting.

Rithik limped down the center of the big boulevard, with Laila on his right and Waro on his left. They passed between canyon walls of metal and glass, stone and light. And beyond the city's edge, where the crooked buildings once more gave way to fields of prehistoric rubble, and the cracked road dwindled into nothing … they came to a vast crevasse.

A cliff stretched across the entire width of the cavern, dropping off into unseen depths. The far side was obscured in impenetrable darkness. But in the center of the cavern, where the road might have gone if it had continued, a natural stone bridge appeared to lead across. From the edge of the cliff, the bridge stretched out into the darkness above the abyss.

There they stopped, as if by an unspoken agreement that this was as far as they would go together.

"Must you go on?" Laila said. "We could find a place to rest in this city."

"There's no time," Rithik said. He could feel the tingle of the ghost flesh clear across his chest and up the back of his head. "I cannot stay here, and there's no going back for me. Unto the end I must go alone."

"I knew you would make it," Waro said.

"What do you mean?"

"Dhat you would find what you're looking for."

"Have I found it?" Rithik said.

"You will." Waro said. "I have a feeling about dhat."

"What about you? Will you stay among the people?"

"For a while anyway. Dhere's a nice spot by a warm spring."

"Goodbye, my friend, and thanks for everything."

"Farewell," Waro said.

Rithik turned to Laila, and she caught his hands in hers. He met the gaze of her large eyes, and she kissed him—a beautiful, bitter sweetness that lingered on his lips.

"Goodbye, Laila."

"Goodbye, Rithik."

Their hands parted, and Rithik took a few steps out onto the bridge, where he paused and looked back.

"I love you both," he said. "I love you all." With that he turned away, but his journey was not over. He had said his goodbyes, but he had not yet reached the end. There was still something out there, on the other side of this bridge. And he had to know what it was. He had to see what it was with his own eyes.

Behind him the city slowly faded into darkness. Ahead, above, and below lay only darkness. He saw only a few feet of the bridge in front of him. From what light and from where he did not know.

As he walked, he shrugged off his vest and dropped it off the side of the bridge. It fell into the abyss without a sound. He unbuckled his belt and dropped that too. He unstrapped the chatter box from his wrist and tossed it over the side. He freed himself of all his gear, and he walked on with nothing but the torn rags that were left of his clothes.

He walked on through the darkness until he saw in the distance a point of light, dead ahead, like the solitary morning star. He walked toward it. The light got bigger, and slowly he began to discern a small stone temple, set among the rocks on the far side.

Where the bridge ended, a path and a few stone steps led up to the temple door. Rithik followed the path, climbed the stairs, pushed open the door, and entered.

He found himself in a small plain room. The walls were white. Soft light surrounded him, but again, from where it came he knew not. It seemed to emanate from the walls, or from the very space before him.

In the middle of the room was a squat octagonal block of stone. Four cables extended from metal fittings on the block, snaked across the floor, and disappeared through cracks in the walls. The center of the stone block must have been hollow, for in it sat a man, his naked shoulders and bald head protruding from an opening on top.

Mini-screens were sewn into the man's eye sockets, in place of eyes. A round speaker was sewn into his mouth. His ears had been folded over and sewn shut. The man seemed alive. His chest rose and fell as he breathed. But he did not acknowledge Rithik's presence.

Rithik approached the man and stood before him. Scenes of horror flashed across the mini-screens. Unimaginable masses of people, suffering and dying from disease, from hunger, and from endless acts of war and violence. Towns flooded. Crops withered. Rivers and oceans poisoned. Entire cities vaporized instantly, obliterated in clouds of fire that mushroomed up toward a blackened sky.

"What is this?" Rithik said. "Who are you?"

But the man made no reply.

Rithik reached out to touch the man, but to his astonishment, his hand passed right through the man's shoulder.

A faint sound emanated from the speaker in the man's mouth, but Rithik couldn't make it out. He bent down and put his ear close to the speaker. He heard a kind of crackle and static.

It sounded like ghost chatter.

A chill crawled up Rithik's spine. On the far side of the room he saw another door. He left the man behind, opened the next door, and went through.

There was another small room, much like the one before. But in the middle of this room was a woman crawling around on the floor. Her naked body had been stripped of skin. All that remained of her face and form was charred fat and muscle and bone, networks of blood vessels, and thousands of exposed nerve endings.

The woman writhed in agony. She seemed to be trying to find something. She groped around on the ground with her bloody hands. She sniffed at the air. And when she couldn't find what she was looking for, she appeared to wail and moan, but no trace of sound reached Rithik's ears.

Rithik walked toward her. When he got close, the woman's hand reached out toward his leg, but passed right through. She looked up. Her lipless teeth chattered. For a moment her wide, blind eyes seemed to look at Rithik.

Then she turned away again, groping the ground in search of something.

Rithik moved on, unable to bear the horrible sight any longer. There was yet another door on the far side of the room. He passed through, and as he did, he realized each preceding room seemed to fade into darkness behind him.

In the center of the next room was an eight-foot high, cylindrical glass tank, standing upright on a round stone dais. The tank was capped with a round stone slab, and filled with a clear fluid through which bubbles slowly rose. Floating submerged in the fluid was a young boy. The top of the boy's scalp and skull had been removed, exposing his brain. A multitude of metallic tubes were inserted into the soft brain matter, and from the tubes, wires extended upward to connections on the underside of the tank's lid. The boy's naked body appeared to be alive, but his face wore an expression of deep sleep. His eyes and mouth were closed, relaxed, and peaceful.

For a long time Rithik stood in front of the tank and studied the boy's face. He seemed strangely familiar. His face stirred within Rithik an emotion he could not name, a feeling he could not define or explain. But no matter how long he looked, he could not imagine who the boy was, nor where he could have remembered him from.

Of course this too, the boy, the liquid, the tank, was also a ghostly illusion with no tangible reality. Eventually

Rithik had to move on. There were no answers for him here. Only an endless stream of thoughts, emotions, images, and nothing more.

Through a final door he passed out of the temple. Beyond, a great mountain rose up, almost touching the stone firmament overhead. The sun and moon seemed to swing in their arcs, phantom-like, beyond the lithic sky. And high on the base of the mountain, Rithik saw the entrance to a cave.

26

YANANNA'S CAVE

He climbed the slope leading up to the base of the mountain, as if guided by an invisible presence. Beneath the light of a ghostly sun, he zig-zagged up toward the mouth of a cave that never escaped his view. He did not rush. He did not linger. And when he reached the entrance, he did not hesitate to enter.

The passage was utterly dark, and he had to feel his way along the stone walls. He had nothing left to lose. All hope and fear had left him. For in the depths of this labyrinth, there was no up or down, no left or right, no inside or outside, no underworld or overworld.

The tunnel led him forward, spiraled inward, and opened into a rocky chamber. A pool of water shimmered in the center of the room, radiating light. In it swirled endless stars and galaxies, heaving in the tides of cosmic space.

On the other side of the pool, standing at its edge, stood the goddess. Black cloth was wrapped about her waist, its trailing end draped over her shoulder. Black hair fell in cascades about her sullen visage. Her bare skin gleamed in the cosmic light.

"Yananna!" Rithik said, unable to utter anything more.

At her feet were four skulls, those of a man, an ubok, a lion, and an eagle.

Yananna's voice reverberated through Rithik's entire being. "I've been waiting for you," she said. "Drink from this water, and you can stay with me here forever."

Rithik gazed into the pool. Within he saw the light of countless worlds, spinning in the endless reaches of space.

"Drink," the goddess said, "and you will be cured."

The lights within the pool danced in a pattern of endless fascination.

"Drink," the goddess said again, "and you will live forever."

But there was no life or death anymore. There was only this … whatever this was.

Rithik looked up, breaking his gaze from the lights in the pool. The goddess awaited his decision, his action, but in the silence something caught Rithik's attention at the side of the chamber. His eye was drawn to the entrance of another dark passage, as if the spiral inward continued there. The tunnel beyond was darker than dark, a kind of void, an emptiness, which drew his gaze ever deeper.

"What's through there?" Rithik said.

"Nothing," the goddess said.

Rithik gazed into the darkness, then back at the goddess.

This too, Rithik realized, was an illusion. These thoughts … these feelings … these memories … these images … were all forms arising in consciousness.

He turned away from the image of the goddess, and walked to the entrance of the dark passage.

He stood at the edge and gazed into nothing.

This was really it then, the end of all things. Beyond this, nothing could be said. There at the threshold of the unknown, his searching finally stopped. He realized, with startling clarity, that this whole world was Yananna's cave. He could not explain it. But with that realization, in waves of unimaginable relief, the last traces of world corruption flowed out of him. He was empty now, as empty as the darkness before him. There was no Rithik anymore, and yet he was aware.

And as he entered the darkness, and went ever deeper, he had the strange sensation that from within it, he would be born.

About the Author

Matthew Lowes is a writer of weird fiction and games. His stories have appeared in a variety of publications, including *Dark Recesses*, *Anotherealm*, and *ShadowSpinners: A Collection of Dark Tales*. He is the designer and author of *Dungeon Solitaire: Labyrinth of Souls* and several other games-related books. He is currently working on a trilogy of fantasy novels, a collection of horror stories, and two roleplaying games. Lowes lives in the beautiful Pacific Northwest where every day he pursues the dreams and ideas that are the inspiration for his work.

matthewlowes.com

The Original
DUNGEON SOLITAIRE
Tomb of Four Kings

Still Available for Free

at

matthewlowes.com/games

Complete Rules
are Print-Ready and Playable
with any Standard Deck
of Playing Cards

Dungeon Solitaire
Labyrinth of Souls

TAROT CARD GAME

by MATTHEW LOWES
Illustrated by JOSEPHE VANDEL

Complete Rulebook
&
Labyrinth of Souls Tarot Deck
Available at
matthewlowes.com/games

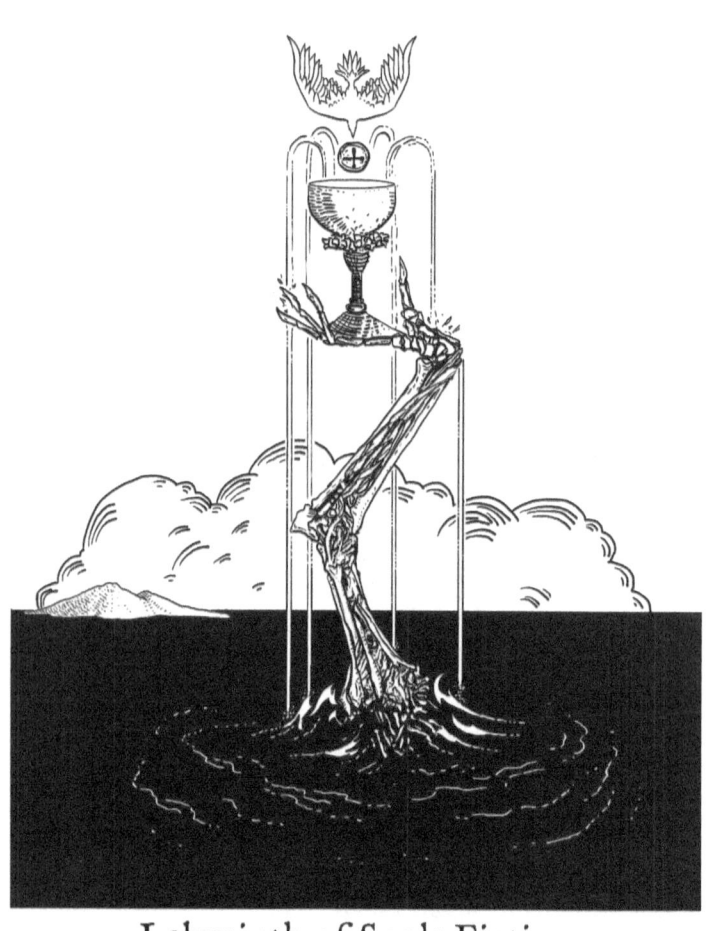

Labyrinth of Souls Fiction
Coming Soon

Littlest Death by Eric Witchey
The Door of Tireless Pursuits by Stephen T. Vessels
Bayou's Lament by Cheryl Owen-Wilson
Exhumation of the Divine by Pamela Jean Herber

... and more to come!

information at
shadowspinnerspress.com